PRAISE FOR EMMA

'... turns playful and poi...
...bstance, this coming-of ag...
...readers from the first page to the last.'
SCHOOL LIBRARIES JOURNAL, STARRED REVIEW

'... a beautifully written story.'
INDEPENDENT ON SUNDAY

'...unny, poignant ... [a] wise and accessible read.'
WALL STREET JOURNAL

'Amber's oddball voice makes the lessons go down easy.'
NEW YORK TIMES

'A funny and heart-warming novel about modern-day
families, starting school, being of mixed race
and celebrating your uniqueness.'
LOVEREADING4KIDS

'... snappily narrated and exuberantly illustrated,
[*Dara Palmer's Major Drama*] is sure to win readers over.'
PUBLISHERS WEEKLY

'... wonderfully modern voice that manages to perfectly
balance a sensitive subject with light and laughter.'
BOOKTRUST

'Fun and thought-provoking.'
...OPLE MAGAZINE

A MESSAGE FROM CHICKEN HOUSE

I've always believed I can talk to animals – and I suppose I can. But the brilliant Emma Shevah has them actually *answer back* – and tell us the truth about our world! Our two lovable misfit heroes, Ivy and Nathaniel, set up the Animal Action Agency to spread their message and change minds. Along the way, they uncover a few unexpected secrets . . . Come on, let's join them – and don't forget to talk to the animals, you never know when they might reply!

BARRY CUNNINGHAM
Publisher
Chicken House

HOW TO SAVE THE WORLD

WITH A CHICKEN AND AN EGG

Emma Shevah

2 Palmer Street, Frome, Somerset BA11 1DS
www.chickenhousebooks.com

Text © Emma Shevah 2021
Illustrations © Kirsti Beautyman 2021

First published in Great Britain in 2021
Chicken House
2 Palmer Street
Frome, Somerset BA11 1DS
United Kingdom
www.chickenhousebooks.com

Cover and interior design by Helen Crawford-White
Cover and inside illustrations by Kirsti Beautyman
Typeset by Dorchester Typesetting Group Ltd
Printed and bound in Great Britain by CPI Group (UK) Ltd, Croydon CR0 4YY

The paper used in this Chicken House book is made from
wood grown in sustainable forests.

1 3 5 7 9 10 8 6 4 2

British Library Cataloguing in Publication data available.

PB ISBN 978-1-910655-47-4
eISBN 978-1-913322-44-1

To the animals of Planet Earth with our humblest apologies and our deepest love.

'After a short time in the country, it was no longer possible for one thoughtlessly to kill a fly, and I have never in the presence of a Tibetan squashed an insect which bothered me. The attitude of the people in these matters is really touching. If at a picnic an ant crawls up one's clothes, it is gently picked up and set down. It is a catastrophe when a fly falls in a cup of tea. It must at all costs be saved from drowning as it may be the reincarnation of one's dead grandmother. In winter they break the ice in the pools to save fishes before they freeze to death, and in summer they rescue them before the pools dry up. These creatures are kept in pails or tins until they can be restored to their home waters. Meanwhile their rescuers have done something for the good of their souls. The more life one can save the happier one is.'

Seven Years in Tibet, **Heinrich Harrer**

'. . . there truly is hope. Other peoples, other species, even other kinds of sea turtles – in situations as bad, sometimes worse – have recovered. Turtles have taught me this: do all you can and don't worry about the odds against you.

Voyage of the Turtle:
In Pursuit of the Earth's Last Dinosaur, **Carl Safina**

'The world is changing because we're changing it. And that makes me understand, at least, what kind of person I'd like to be. A person can seek ways, whether big or small, to heal the world.

'One doesn't wait for a revolution. One becomes it.'

The View from Lazy Point:
A Natural Year in an Unnatural World, **Carl Safina**

I. IVY

It's hard telling a story. There's never really a beginning. Something always happened before the part you *think* is the beginning, and there are all these details you need to add so everyone understands the whole set-up. The beginning of this story was probably when the world was formed, creatures started walking around and humans decided they were boss, but I can't start there because it'll take way too long. And I can't start with the strange feeling I had inside that *something huge was coming*, or the night on the beach when it actually came and the impossible possible happened. No. Important things happened before that night. So I should probably start by saying I can talk to animals.

Yes. You heard correctly.

This doesn't mean I blab at them and they stare at me blankly, wondering who this weird human is and

3

when I'll shut up and give them food. I mean I understand them like I *am* them. Like I've *zshoomed* inside their brain and they've *zshoomed* inside mine. Which *can* be awesome, but it can also be heartbreaking and land me in big trouble.

I don't know when it started. I must have been very small because one of my earliest memories is of being a duck. This was before I knew I was a human, and before Daddy Jeremy explained that my skin was where I ended and the rest of the world began. The way I saw it in my baby brain, life was one big whirl of colour and smell and noise that somehow included me.

I was watching Polly at the time. When I was a duck, I mean. She was an Indian Runner, which is a breed of duck that has a long neck and waddles but can't fly. She could quack, though, and not all ducks are quackers. Most male ducks are completely silent, which is just as well because you should hear the females. Shocking moaners, ducks. Mind you, they've got good reason, what with their habitats being destroyed and their ducklings being feisty little bigmouths and everything.

Most ducks live for ten years, but Polly only lived for five because a fox nabbed her and left a trail of brown and white feathers where Polly used to be. I did like Polly, but she sprayed liquid poo everywhere

4

so she wasn't the best pet if you wanted a clean yard or a clean baby. Not that I noticed. Right then, my eyes were fixed on her bobbing up and down as she ate oats in front of my upturned toes, and that's when it happened.

She lifted her head and looked at me. I looked at her. Everything else went *zshooom* and out of focus. Her mind sank into mine and we sort of . . . merged and became one. I could feel this hazy glow where the two of us zinged together in a duck/girl mishmash, with no edges or borders or rims.

Later, I figured out I wasn't a duck at all. The time had to come sooner or later, I suppose. How could I be a duck when I was also a dog, an ant, a starfish, a spider, a seagull, a horse and a crab? Because that merge thing? It started happening with other animals as well. All of them. Even *snails*. And it kept happening.

When I found out I was human it was a huge shock. Huge.

It's nice being a duck. I recommend it if you ever get the chance. It's fun being lots of creatures, actually, except they all have their problems, and some more than others. I have them, too, of course. My main number one problem is that I want to save the world and I have no idea how to do it because the world is extremely massive, full of crazy people, and I'm not even twelve yet.

I wouldn't even know where to begin because that's not a subject we're taught at school, even though you'd think that would be the most vitally crucial thing we could ever learn. And there aren't any 'How to Save the World When You're Eleven' type books in the library. I know because I've checked.

All I know is that animals need me. But what are you supposed to do when you're only eleven and you don't have a jeep or money or veterinary skills? I have to sit around, knowing whole species are endangered, suffering and dying, and I can't do a single thing about it. I mean, obviously, I give sugar solution to tired bees, leave seeds out for hungry birds and go on slug- and snail-moving missions on rainy nights with rubber gloves on to stop them getting squished, but everyone does that. Some people even do it *without* rubber gloves on.

But what I really want to do is save creatures. All of them. And the coral and the seas and the forests and the air. Which is a mission, I admit, but it needs to be done. I can't just sit around and watch everything die.

If people don't believe me then fine, whatever – it only bothers me because it interferes with my ability to save the world. No one listens to you if they think you're making things up. They get mean about it too.

It makes my blood fizz when humans are horrible to animals, but when they're bad to each other? Seriously, what is *that*?

Unfortunately, I've experienced this myself, so I stay away from humans and do small acts of kindness to help animals have a better life. Just to, you know, pass the time until I get old enough to do something world-changingly serious. But while I was passing time until I could do something world-changingly serious, something world-changingly serious happened. Something impossible. Obviously it *wasn't* impossible, because it happened, which means it *was* possible. It was an impossible thing that couldn't possibly happen, but somehow, impossibly, did.

Look, it makes total sense to me. And it will to you too in the end (hopefully).

This story isn't about ducks, by the way. It's about secrets, the seaside, and how seagulls trick worms into thinking it's raining. It's also about mucus, fudge and dogs needing a wider variety of sniffs. But if you want the simple version, it's about what happened here last summer. It involves animals too – lots of them – and an unusual boy called Nathaniel with a mystery to solve. So we should probably start with him.

2. NATHANIEL

It did not start well.

I told him about exploding ants and he *still* ignored me. Who isn't interested in exploding ants?

Rory Hewitt, that's who.

Uncle Charles was paying him to take me from my boarding school in Harrow to my mother's house in Suffolk for the first two weeks of the summer holidays. I did not want some unknown colleague's unknown son to collect me from school because that wasn't usual, and I liked usual. And I certainly did not want to stay with my mother. I barely knew her. I hadn't even seen her since I was four because she and Grandma didn't get on.

I wanted Grandma to collect me, as she always did, and take me to her home in Dorset. To my cosy bed with the soft white sheets. To the wooden snail house I made when I was six. To the rooms I loved, full of books, carvings, paintings and rugs that Grandma had brought back from her travels. But I wouldn't be going there or seeing Grandma ever again, which was impossible to comprehend, like trying to grasp the limitlessness of the universe, only infinitely sadder.

Instead, I was going to stay with my mother.

'Being chaperoned by a nineteen-year-old will be fun,' my housemaster said. 'Be at reception at 9.05 a.m. on Friday and Rory will meet you there. Do you have your rubber . . . er . . . squeezers?'

I nodded. 'A red ball in my left pocket to squeeze when I feel especially uneasy, and a blue one in my right for when I'm just a bit on edge.'

'Excellent.'

'Can I tell Rory about mucus?'

Mr Upcott's cheek twitched. 'Er . . . perhaps not *initially*. You'll say hello, shake his hand, and then laugh all the way to Suffolk, ordering each of the snacks on the refreshment trolley.'

'I only like Double Deckers. And some trains don't have refreshment trolleys.'

'Nathaniel . . .'

'Oh. You aren't being literal.'

'Exactly.'

I nodded, even though I didn't understand. Being literal makes perfect sense. Why propose something that may never happen?

And it didn't. At 9.17 a.m., a tall boy with elongated nostrils strode into the reception area and mumbled a curt hello. He had blond floppy hair, and wore a blue shirt, jeans and tan shoes studded with little holes. I didn't see any socks, which looked uncomfortable. I wanted to ask if it was, but he was twelve minutes late and he didn't shake my hand, both of which confused me. I lifted mine, to show him what was *supposed* to happen, but then lowered it again when he unscrewed the lid of a plastic water bottle.

My eyes widened. 'It takes four hundred and fifty years for those to decompose,' I informed him. 'Some take a thousand years.'

'Fascinating,' he said, closing the lid.

He didn't *seem* fascinated, so I added, 'British people buy 2.8 bottles of water each week. If they switched to reusable bottles, in one year it would save enough plastic to reach to the moon and back.'

He flared his nostrils and muttered, 'This is going to be fun.'

I nodded in agreement, even though he didn't seem to fully grasp the harm caused by plastic bottles. I'd tell him again later in the journey, multiple times if necessary.

He signed me out of school and strode ahead,

rolling my suitcase behind him. He was practically running, even though it was already nearly twenty-nine degrees outside. When I tried to reach him, he sped up, so I sped up too, which made me trip over my feet and fall on the pavement. It hurt, and because he stopped and glared, I was embarrassed. But then I noticed some ants teeming between the cracks. I felt awkward, so I said, 'A species of carpenter ant in Asia called *Colobopsis saundersi* can make itself explode to protect its nest from intruders.' Rory walked on so I hobbled after him. He stopped to cross the road, so I did too, speaking louder to be heard over the traffic. 'You probably know that the salivary glands in the jaw are called mandibular glands, and that's why the lower jaw is called the mandible?'

He didn't nod. He just monitored the passing traffic.

'Well, the ants have two large mandibular glands running all the way down their bodies, and they're filled with poison instead of saliva. Spit, basically. Poisonous spit.'

Rory gave me a sideways glance. 'I know what saliva is.'

I squeezed my red rubber ball and smiled. I'd been practising smiling by holding a toothbrush between my teeth and looking in the mirror. I didn't have one in my teeth then, of course, but it may have looked that way: I hadn't really mastered it yet. Unimpressed, Rory crossed the road and I followed, narrowly avoiding a man in Lycra on a speeding bike.

Uncle Charles taught me never to surrender, so I soldiered on. 'When intruders enter the nest, the ant attacks them —' I added, raising my voice because the cyclist was now yelling at me — 'but if it's losing the fight, it violently contracts the muscles in its abdomen and ruptures its body, breaking open the mandibular gland and spraying poison in all directions.'

I waited for Rory's reaction. He had to be impressed with that. *Colobopsis saundersi* were high on the list of creatures I most wanted to see.

But Rory was not impressed.

I was crushed. We had a three-hour journey ahead and I very much wanted to talk to someone. Uncle Charles and Aunt Nancy had returned to East Sussex after Grandma's funeral, and I'd returned to school, but no one talked to me there. I wasn't sure why. I was only too happy to tell them all kinds of intriguing facts. Perhaps Grandma was right: it takes time to find like-minded people.

But something else had been bothering me, too. In her hospital room before she died, Grandma whispered that she had something important to tell me. She was agitated. She mentioned it only when we were alone.

'I should never have . . . your mother . . . you must . . . know that . . . your mother . . . she . . .'

'. . . is a pig?' I offered, when I saw she was running out of breath. It wasn't an insult in the slightest: pigs are the second most intelligent creatures on the planet after chimpanzees – dolphins only come third. Pigs are as intelligent as three-year-old humans. Not many people know that, which makes pigs unexpectedly interesting, and I was hoping my mother would be the same.

Grandma never told me why my mother couldn't look after me. I knew she lived in India because I wrote to her there. I assumed she was an intrepid explorer, and she must have been eccentric as well, because Uncle Charles and Aunt Nancy rolled their eyes a lot when they spoke about her, which Mr Upcott taught me is a sign of irritation.

I waited by Grandma's hospital bed for her to tell me more, but by then she was in and out of consciousness. She died the next morning.

What had she wanted to tell me? Was it good or bad?

The next day, at the funeral parlour, Uncle Charles held out a letter in a sealed envelope. 'Grandma wrote this for you, Nathaniel. She's written letters to your mother and Nancy, too. She asked me to give it to you . . . after she . . . you know.' He cleared his throat.

'Charles,' Aunt Nancy said, reaching for it, 'I don't think Nathaniel is ready for that.'

'Nonsense,' Charles said. 'Nathaniel is exceptionally mature, and in any case, she wrote it for him. Here.' He held the letter out and I took it.

Aunt Nancy stood up abruptly and said, 'Nathaniel, would you give us a moment? And perhaps don't open it just yet.'

I left the room and sat in the waiting area. I could hear them arguing from the other side of the chapel of rest. I held the letter to the light but couldn't decipher the words through the thick envelope. I gazed at my name, written in Grandma's coiled handwriting, and decided to slit it open.

Once I'd read it, I stood up and walked back in. They stopped talking when they saw the open letter in my hand, and Aunt Nancy looked at me in a way I couldn't fathom. I stood near the door and mumbled, 'I'd . . . I'd like to stay with my mother . . . during the summer holidays.' What I didn't mention was that Grandma had asked me to in her letter. She said there was something there for me. Something important. She didn't say what, but I intended to discover what it was.

Uncle Charles, Aunt Nancy and my mother looked at each other and I wished I knew what the look meant. Not understanding facial expressions makes life very difficult to comprehend. Nancy did a single, brisk nod, my mother smiled and Uncle Charles said, decisively, 'If that's your wish, then you shall stay with your mother for first two weeks, after which you will come and stay with us until school resumes.' I was glad. I liked their tidy estate. They were ordered, regimented people and their fridge was full of bewildering ingredients that I didn't eat but enjoyed examining in detail.

I returned to school after Grandma's funeral, but I couldn't sleep properly for months. Being tired and worried isn't the best way to make new friends. I still hadn't made any when Year 7 ended, the summer holidays arrived, and I was taken by a boy I'd never met before to stay with a mother I barely knew.

When we reached the station, I was hot and out of breath and so was Rory. Huffing and grunting, he lifted my case up the stairs.

He was not the chaperone I'd been hoping for.

'Go through,' he sneered. I tapped my Oyster card on the yellow reader beside the wider gate, the one where people with buggies and suitcases can enter without being chomped by the mandibles of the ticket barrier. Which reminded me . . . 'Being able to explode your own organs is called autothysis,' I said as he checked the digital noticeboard on the platform. 'It means "self-sacrifice" in Greek. The ants basically sacrifice themselves to save their colony.'

Rory groaned. 'Listen, Little Lord Twitface—'

'My name is Nathaniel and I'm not technically a lor—'

'I've been paid to chaperone you, not have a cosy *tête-à-tête* with you, so shut up about ants, all right? Do we have an understanding?'

I frowned. I didn't understand *at all*. Getting someone's name wrong is rude. And autothysis is incredibly interesting. It's common in superorganisms who work collectively and put the needs of the colony before themselves. Amazonian ants also defend and improve the health of the trees they live on. If humans were superorganisms and put what's best for our species and our habitat first, Earth wouldn't be in this mess.

Maybe Rory just didn't like ants. I squeezed my red ball (this journey, Rory, and the thought of my mother at the other end were all extremely unsettling), and said, 'Some *termite* species use autothysis as well—'

'I *said* shut it!'

'That wasn't about ants!'

His eyes blazed. I think he was angry. 'Fine,' I

mumbled. 'Fine.'

I watched the Tube train pull in, wondering how fast it could go, why it needed a driver at all when it could probably drive automatically, and whether there were mice on the tracks like there were at Tottenham Court Road station. I'd forgotten to look, and there was no one to ask. Certainly not Rory.

I sat beside him, nervous about meeting my mother, confused about having no friends, and baffled about Grandma's letter and what she'd wanted to tell me before she died. Rory slotted his earphones into his ears and listened to music all the way to Liverpool Street, where we boarded the train to Suffolk. Aunt Nancy always says, 'You're never alone with a book, Nathaniel,' so to pass the time, I opened *Planet in Crisis*. It was very informative about the most urgent environmental issues, but it didn't tell readers what to do to bring about change. As I gazed out of the window at the serene, bucolic countryside of rolling fields and farms, I realized two things:

1. Telling people facts and statistics probably isn't enough.

And 2. There's only so much you can learn about in books.

3. IVY

I love books. They teach you everything.

Even though I knew that, I still sat in class that Friday not listening to Miss Vickery at all. Obviously, Ancient Egypt *is* interesting, but how could I focus on dead mummies when I could feel and hear a living creature getting closer and closer every day? When something *that* special and rare happens, you have to tune in to it. So I did. I felt the echo and hum of deep open emptiness and an inner push to keep going. I heard a flap and a lap, and I saw endless blues dotted with sprinkles of sunlight.

Excitedly, I looked around the classroom, trying not to shriek. No one else seemed to notice – they were all listening to Miss Vickery read about Tutankhamun. But the creature was big and beautiful, a long way from home and *coming our way*.

I had to prepare!

As Miss Vickery talked about tombs and curses, I closed my eyes and told the creature, *I'm here Come. I'll do everything I can to help you. I, Ivy Pink Floyd, lay down my life for you. I will be the best (human) friend you could ever want. You can trust me 100%.*

'Ivy,' Miss Vickery said, 'is everything all right?'

I opened my eyes and nodded. 'Headache,' I lied.

'Put your head on the table if you like, but keep listening.'

I crossed my arms on the table, lay my head on them and swallowed hard. I couldn't really be trusted 100%. I'd had a few disasters lately. Jake's goldfish had been unhappy for a while. They'd outgrown their small pond, and when goldfish feel trapped, they'll deliberately overeat till they die, just to get out of there. I told Jake to move them to a bigger pond but he didn't, and then it was too late. (The goldfish told me they were unhappy before they died – I don't communicate with goldfish ghosts, although I'd be fine with that.) This is why I regularly post envelopes of sheep droppings through Jake's letterbox. It won't bring his fish back, but it does make me feel a tiny bit better.

Then there was Misty. Rabbits don't like being in the garden in winter – they'd much rather be on the sofa eating spinach and watching TV. I felt sorry for Misty, so I sneaked into Harriet's garden one cold night, and took Misty home to watch *Magical Creatures* with me. Harriet went to check on her the next morning and thought Misty had been taken by a fox that could open hatch doors, which tells you how not-very-clever Harriet is. Daddy Jeremy made me give Misty back or she'd still be on my sofa now.

To prove to the creature (and to myself, to be honest) that I was reliable, I gave Percy half my crisps at break so I could visit her hamster, Joey, after school. Percy's real name is Persephone McGuire, but she'll give you a Chinese burn if you call her Persephone. Her hair is the colour of a ginger tom's, and she has so many freckles on her face that there are more freckles than face. She's OK and everything, but she's not very good at making the world a better place for creatures.

Anyhow, Joey's cage was worse than I'd expected. It was small anyway, but now he had no chewy snacks, his running wheel had broken, and the water bottle was thick with algae. Worse than that, it was dirty and smelt of acid wee and poo-filled socks.

I ground my teeth. No one should have to live like that. If you're not going to take care of a creature properly, you shouldn't have one. It's just wrong.

Joey was huddled in a corner, but when I said hello, he perked up and stuck his twitchy nose out of the bars. He's small and brown, and he'd have been cute if he didn't look so miserable. I cleared my head and concentrated on him. The rest of the world went *schhhhuuuppp* and we kind of *zshoomed* into each other's brains.

He had a lot to complain about. He showed me pictures of his problems (mental pictures, I mean, not photos from his little hamster album, although that would have been fun).

'He's in a really bad way!' I said to Percy, practising how to keep my head on in infuriating circumstances, which is a good life skill (or so I hear).

'Don't start with the Dolittle stuff,' she said, standing in the doorway with her blue eyes flaming. 'Not with me.'

'He's too hot because his cage is near the heater. And a dog jumps on it.'

'Fang,' she said. 'Uncle Raymond's dog. You know that already, so don't pretend you're, like, channelling the hamster or something.'

'Joey's scared.'

'Yeah, well, Fang isn't called Fang for nothing.'

'No, no,' I said in a panic. 'This is no good. He needs to be off the floor and away from the heater.' I lifted his cage and said, 'Let's put him in the sitting room.'

'Mum said he has to stay here cos he smells.'

'His *cage* smells because you don't clean it!' I yelled.

She took the cage out of my hands and put it back on the floor. 'He's my hamster, Ivy. And stop acting like you can talk to him, cos I won't stick up for you any more.'

I bit my tongue between my teeth so I wouldn't shout, and eventually said in a calmish voice, 'OK, but you need to move his cage.'

'Can't.'

'So clean it! He's not drinking because of the algae, so he's dehydrated, and he can't sleep because his cage stinks. He deserves better than this.'

Percy tossed her head. 'Fine. Later. Let's watch *Scooby Doo*.'

Tears stung my eyes. I loved *Scooby Doo* but I loved Joey more. I reached for the water bottle and Joey nudged my hand through the bars. *Take me with you. Put me in your pocket. Don't leave me here*, he begged. Before you ask, 'What, can Joey speak English?' it's more ... words enter your mind, the same as when an inner voice says, *Maybe putting that cockroach in Hattie's bag isn't the best way to teach her to love insects, Ivy.*

I stroked Joey's head. *It doesn't work like that in the human world*, I explained. *You're not my hamster.* Joey twitched his nose in panic. I gazed into his little black eyes to calm him down. *I'll change your water and check on you tomorrow. If nothing's changed, I'll get you out of here. OK?*

He sniffed. Hamsters don't understand 'tomorrow' or 'yesterday'. Most animals don't – they're very here and now. Some store food, so they must have some idea what the future is, but 'I'll come back tomorrow' isn't easy for a hamster to stuff in its cheeks for later.

I had to go home: Daddy Jeremy didn't know where I was and I didn't want to worry him. I rubbed the algae off the bottle with their pan scourer, filled it with fresh water and slotted it back. 'Percy, clean his cage! And find somewhere else to put him. Please.'

'You sound like my mum. Bye, Ivy. See ya.'

I felt ill. *I'll be back*, I said to Joey. *I promise*. He curled up in the corner of his cage, breaking my heart into a thousand spindly pieces.

'You're so weird!' Percy bellowed as I opened the front door.

'Thank you,' I said, as I closed it behind me. Because being weird has its advantages.

Three hours later, Percy knocked at my door.

I froze when I saw her face. I can see pictures in animals' minds, but I can't see a thing in humans' minds: they need to spell it out to me. 'What?' I asked. 'How's Joey?'

23

'Fang came over after you left.'

'Is Joey OK? PERCY! TELL ME!'

'He's dead, Ivy.'

That was the worst moment of my entire life.

When we buried Joey in Percy's mum's flowerbed my insides went cold as rabbit droppings in the freezer (not relevant). I was furious with Percy, but it was my fault too. Joey had told me how scared he was and I'd left him there to die. I cried the most painful lung-crushing eye-stinging heart-arching cry I'd ever cried. Percy even cried for three or four seconds, and she *never* cries. She still didn't believe me, though. She thought it was just a coincidence.

Poor Joey. He didn't understand that the human world has strange rules. You can't walk out of your friend's house with her pet in your pocket. Her parents will call your parents and you'll get in trouble. No one considers it an act of mercy, a rescue mission or a heroic attempt to save a life.

But that was it: with the creature coming, and Joey's death sitting on me like an overweight adult water buffalo, I had to prove to animals that I was on their side.

The animal kingdom needed me. I wasn't going to let it down, I just needed to try harder.

4. NATHANIEL

Rory wasn't trying very hard. It's not *that* difficult to be friendly – at least, that's what my housemaster told me after I spent the first term frowning. In the second term, he taught me the toothbrush-smiling technique. I think it had the opposite effect, but at least I made an effort.

'I don't like you,' I told Rory. He didn't reply, but then he did have his headphones on. I sat beside him feeling more alone than I'd felt in a long while. More alone than when my classmates left for the holidays and I sat waiting for someone I didn't know to take me to a place I didn't want to go to. More alone than I felt in my bed every night, trying to imagine the rest of my life without Grandma.

I squeezed my blue ball and read another paragraph.

The top ten issues facing humans today are:

1. Climate change
2. Ecosystems and endangered species
3. Deforestation
4. Pollution
5. Water scarcity and water pollution
6. Loss of biodiversity
7. Overpopulation
8. Waste disposal
9. Land management and urban sprawl
10. Unhealthy environments and public health

I shook my head. Surely that was the same single problem broken into ten parts? I continued reading.

The best way to curtail negative climate change is to build sustainably, reduce fossil fuels, use renewable energy sources such as solar and wind power, and limit waste and pollution to help preserve the environment.

We have the knowledge, skills and technologies to create positive rather than negative climate change.

I looked up. Humans had done this, and humans could fix it. We still had time.

Much as I wanted to, I didn't share that encouraging fact with Rory.

'Your mother's sending a car,' Rory said when we arrived at Darsham, two hours later. 'I've been asked to wait, but you'll be perfectly fine. If anyone tries to kidnap you, you could always rupture your abdominal muscles and explode.'

At least he'd been paying attention. Sort of.

'I'm not an ant,' I said.

'Not sure I agree.'

Well, that was mean.

At the funeral, Uncle Charles told me men don't cry. That's clearly nonsense: crying is a natural human response to emotions and it helps remove irritants from the eye. My eyes were irritant-free, but I bit my lip because I didn't want Rory to make fun of me, and he was the kind of person who would.

He finished drinking and threw the bottle in a bin.

'Humans use a million plastic bottles a minute,' I said, because even when you're sad, you still have to do the right thing. '91% of them won't be recycled.'

Rory grunted. 'What do you want me to do with it, Einstein? Eat it?'

'I'm called Nathaniel. And yes, preferably.'

'*What?*'

'In 2019, London Marathon runners drank water from edible seaweed pouches instead of the 919,000 plastic bottles they used the year before . . .' I stopped talking because he looked angry.

'That bottle wasn't seaweed, though, was it? Stupid. Little. Weed.' He slammed my suitcase down and strode towards the opposite platform to get the train back to London. He didn't even say goodbye.

I stood in the car park area, my schoolbag on my damp back, and squeezed my red *and* my blue balls simultaneously. It didn't help that much, so I started counting.

Despite the heatwave, storm clouds were gathering. People with pink skin drove up to meet family and friends, and hugged each other warmly, making it look easy. The 17.49 London train arrived, and presumably Rory got on it. Once he'd left, I felt even worse. The people picking up their loved ones drove away. Traffic trundled past on the main road, causing more air pollution.

No one came for me.

I swallowed. Would I be there all day? What would I do when it became dark? What if I stood there all week? Or all summer?

After four minutes, a taxi rolled into the parking area. The driver lowered the window. He had grey skin and looked a bit dead. A wasp hovered near his open window and he hit it with the back of his hand. It ricocheted on to the ground and I shrank. Wasp venom contains a pheromone that causes other wasps to become more aggressive, so you don't want to irritate them near their hive. My eleventh favourite saliva fact is that they chew up strips of bark and spit them out to form a rough paper to make their nests. I'd love to have made my own home from spit, but I didn't have the skills or the right type of saliva.

'Breakwell, are ya?' the driver asked slowly. The wasp recovered and flew away. 'Gon'a Southwold? Lady Huntington?'

'Yes.'

'G'in, then.'

I didn't get in.

He climbed out of the driver's seat and lifted my suitcase into the boot. 'An'thing wrong?'

'Your car isn't electric. A two-mile drive puts two pounds of CO_2 into the atmosphere.'

He rubbed his chin. 'Right. Well, I in't got no 'lectric car, so you coming wi'me or staying here?'

Rain sprinkled on to my glasses. I don't like getting wet unless I'm swimming or in the bath, and I was already uncomfortably damp from the heat. The driver sat back in his non-electric car. My suitcase was in the boot and the rain was getting stronger.

I opened the door and got in. Then I felt even more nervous. Cars suck in harmful fumes, so being inside doesn't protect you from pollution. You can be exposed to eight times more than a cyclist if you don't use the recycled air setting on the fan. His fan was not set on recycled air. And isn't getting into a stranger's car something you should never, ever do? Didn't taxi drivers count as strangers? Which strangers were OK and which weren't?

A squashed hedgehog lay by the road, which reminded me. 'Hedgehogs have around five thousand spines,' I said. 'Each lasts for a year, then it drops out and a replacement grows. They don't all fall out at the same time. No one's seen a bald hedgehog.'

His dead eyes fixed on mine in the rear-view mirror. I squeezed my red ball. 'If hedgehogs smell or taste something strong,' I added, 'they cover their spines in foamy saliva. No one knows why.' I know lots of facts about bodily fluids. Mucus and saliva are my favourites. He turned the radio on. Maybe he wasn't a hedgehog fan. Maybe exploding ants were more his thing. 'A species of carpenter ant in Malaysia—' I began.

He turned the volume up. I couldn't compete with the radio, even though I tried. We reached Southwold two minutes after I finished saying, '. . . and sprays poison in all directions.' My face burnt with heat and shame. I thought I was communicating perfectly but people just didn't interact with me.

I looked at the high street, crisscrossed with bunting. Children in shorts and stripy T-shirts walked with their families and I thought how nice that must be. Then I remembered I was going to stay with my mother for the first time in years. The last time I saw her, she was leaving for India in tears, Grandma was angry with her and I didn't understand why either of those things were happening. Meanwhile, I was more interested in playing mini golf, which was next on Grandma's timetable, than hugging my crying mother.

But now I was on my way to her house for two whole weeks.

I opened the window to get some air and squeezed the red ball until my knuckles went white.

Then I saw her. Not my mother – a girl my age. She was walking along a side road, her long black hair flapping, her bright blue T-shirt and denim shorts baring dark arms and legs. She had a brown chicken wedged under her arm, which she was chatting to like it was the most normal thing in the world. A black Labrador plodded behind her with no lead. The girl stopped beside a ginger cat, bent down and tilted her head to one side. Then she nodded slowly, as if she were listening to it, tilted her head and then opened her mouth wide and started singing. To the cat.

She turned her head as she sang, and caught me staring at her. She frowned. I was frowning too, for obvious reasons. I've read that a giraffe's hair is ten times thicker than human hair, elephants mourn their dead, and the cry of the blue whale is the loudest sound of all creatures and can be heard five hundred miles away. But no book has ever revealed whether a cat likes being sung to by a girl carrying a chicken.

5. IVY

These disasters couldn't carry on. I had to prove to the animal world that I was completely trustworthy and I would be there for every creature always.

So I took Dot to the library after Joey's funeral even though it wasn't our usual library day. I needed to find books on saving creatures when human owners get in the way, but I also needed to be kinder, and taking your hen to the library is a kind thing to do. Hens love the library. Dot told me so herself. She's an Orpington hen and they never lie – it's just not in their nature. Ever met an Orpington that works as a secret agent? Exactly. Now you know why.

Dot's a good listener, even if she can't keep her head still, and you can't say that about everyone. My dog, Daddy Rufus, is my other best friend. He's a good listener as well, but his head stays so still sometimes, I think he's fallen asleep (probably has). I call him Daddy Rufus because he's like a father to me. Which means I have three fathers now: my birth father, Daddy Jeremy (my foster father) and Daddy Rufus. Even though Daddy Rufus's breath smells of sardines, when I hugged him for the first time, so much love and strength and wisdom flowed from him that all the nastiness of my real father almost melted away. Almost. All children should have dog parents if their human ones aren't nice to them. It should be the law.

I was telling you about the trip to the library. I get distracted. It happens to me all the time. People say I don't know the difference between what's relevant and what isn't. You know what I think? Rubbish. Everything is relevant. Everything. Even the things I don't think are relevant turn out to be relevant, and I think *everything* is relevant. Daddy Jeremy tells me all the time, 'I do believe you're digressing again, my dear. Could you possibly stick to the point so I can follow your train of thought?' At 'Teacher Evening' (they don't call it 'Parents' Evening' any more because not all children live with their parents), my teachers complain to Jeremy and Aisling about it. Obviously, I'll try to stick to the most relevantly relevant parts of this story or I'll be telling it for ever. Not promising anything, though. Just so you know.

Relevant: Rufus and I are the same age, but I'm still young and he's old now, which is weird. I don't put him on a lead and he doesn't put me on one, and we're both happy about that. When I tell him my problems, he looks at me, sighs and puts his head on his paws. He's the quiet type so he's not great at advice, but he's still my best friend. I love having best friends that are animals. I have no idea why you'd ever need a human one.

Anyhow. Wendy the librarian makes me leave Dot on the low wall outside. I tell Wendy all the time that Dot likes being inside, surrounded by books of all kinds, because she likes stories as much as I do. But hens are not great sitter-downers and Dot gets over-excited and clucks a lot. Wendy doesn't have a hen best friend, so she just doesn't get it. Who cares about a calm, quiet library when you can have a happy hen?

Dot and I took a detour, of course. I needed to check on the ants near the lighthouse and see if the robin was feeling more at home in his new nest in the oak. But I felt worse than ever. The huge thing was coming, and all I'd done lately was fail animals.

Unfortunately, I spent so long getting to the library, it was closed when I got there, which was another fail, but at least this time, no creatures died in the process (thankfully). It wasn't the first time Dot and I have arrived after Wendy's locked up. It's hard keeping to opening hours when creatures you meet along the way don't have any idea of clocks or time. Dot was annoyed, but I told her we'd go back tomorrow.

I did manage to do one kind deed, though.

On the way back home, I saw Wendy's cat, Misha, sitting under the tree. I couldn't *properly* help her: Misha wanted kittens and couldn't have any, so I sang 'Love is all you need' to make her feel better. Cats like love songs. Misha likes Russian ones, but I don't know any, so sometimes I sing in a Russian accent, but Misha thinks I sound like a Hungarian otter with a toothache. Charming. 'Least I try.

While I was singing, I caught a boy staring at me from a car window. I made a face at him, then the car turned the corner and he was gone. Then Dot squawked and got in a huge flap (she literally flaps, unlike me) so I calmed her down with a limerick about a fox getting its head bitten off (not relevant). Then I remembered how excited she'd been about the library, so I told her I'd read her an extra story tomorrow, to make up for it.

She was happy with that.

Sometimes it takes a chicken to remind us humans of the important things in life.

6. NATHANIEL

A cat sat by a gate, looking rather important, as we stopped outside the Red Lion pub. I could smell the salt air even from the road.

'Let's be 'avin' you, then,' the driver said, opening his door. I didn't know what that meant. Was he going to eat me? He lifted my suitcase from the boot and said, 'House is up there.' He pointed to a hill with cannons along the top. I would have asked about them but the taxi driver was not the illuminating type. On the left was a dilapidated manor house, even grander than Grandma's in Dorset, with a sign on the wall saying 'Huntington House', and a greying statue of a woman with no clothing on in the tangled front garden. I looked away, squeezing my blue ball, and heard a voice cry, 'Nathaniel!'

My stomach clenched.

My mother was running down the path, her feral

brown hair pushed back by orange plastic sunglasses. Her top was wrinkled and green, and her loose trousers were brown, so she looked a little like a tree in the wind. Her eyes seemed a brighter blue now she was tanned, and she was smiling, which of course she hadn't been doing at the funeral a few months before. She moved in a brisk, efficient manner and although she was welcoming, she also seemed confused, as though she'd recently lost her head and had been frantically searching everywhere for it, only to realize that it had been on her neck all along.

She did not look like an intrepid explorer.

'You're here!' she said. 'Wonderful! Boy?'

Maybe she was checking, so I replied. 'Yes. I'm a boy.'

She tittered like a tinkling piano. 'I was asking where the other one was.'

'Which oth—?'

'Chaperone fellow.'

'Oh. He left me at Darsham and went back to London.'

She frowned. 'He was employed to bring you to my door. I shall have words. Thank you, Colin. Gorgeous tomato chutney.'

I couldn't see any chutney, but the driver smiled. 'I'll tell Gwen. She'll be happy.'

'Can't find the jar, of course,' she went on. 'Chaos as usual in there.' She chuckled and didn't notice my look of horror. *Chaos?*

'It'll turn up. You're a national treasure, Colin,' she added.

Colin beamed. 'Don't know 'bout that.' He glanced at me and muttered, ''lectric cars.'

My mother handed him the fare and said, 'Please don't insult me by giving me change.'

'Much obliged, Lady H.'

'Oh, please call me Henny. Can't bear the whole ...'

'Right you are. Pleasure as always.'

I watched my mother with alarm. I could see why Grandma didn't get on with her. She was eccentric, unpredictable and scatty, and Grandma could not abide those characteristics in a human being. She also seemed spontaneous, rambunctious and messy, and those were very much the opposite of our orderly lifestyle. I liked tidiness and timetables. Sequences and schedules. Regulation and routine. They made me feel safe. Not chaotic homes where jam jars went missing.

I wanted to leave on the next train, like Rory, and travel to Uncle Charles and Aunt Nancy's house. But as Grandma had asked me specifically to come here, I would stay for two weeks. Surely I could do that.

I would find whatever it was Grandma said was here for me, and then I'd leave.

Nervously, I followed my mother towards the house. Once in, she shut the front door, faced me and wrinkled her eyes. I wasn't sure whether that meant she was sad, disgusted, or had eaten something spicy and was about to burp.

'Let's have a look at you, then. Growing into a fine young man, I see. I suppose a boy of your age doesn't want a hug from his long-lost mother,' she said, 'so I won't embarrass you. Come on in.'

Thank goodness. Physical contact made me very uncomfortable. Fortunately the members of my family tended to touch each other only in times of medical emergency. I left my suitcase near the door and followed her along the hallway.

It really was chaotic. My head felt as if it were being crushed in a giant nutcracker, so I squeezed the red ball repeatedly and tried not to panic. The green hallway was cluttered with furniture, and in the sitting room there was a long table covered in piles and piles of papers. Two dogs, a small, shaggy one with black fur and a large white-haired beast, bounded towards us with their tails wagging, mouths panting, and claws scratching the wooden floor. I can't read dogs' expressions very well, either, and I seized up in case they bit me. I know lots of facts about animals, but I find it hard to tell if dogs are serious with their barks or just trying to make a point.

'Kitchen!' my mother snapped, pointing down the hallway. The dogs scampered off, which was just as well because I thought she was talking to me. 'This is the sitting room,' she said, standing by the doorway.

I peeked in. It was strewn with boxes, contraptions, cushions, lever arch folders, plants and shawls. Paintings of intricate circles, and photos of ancient temples covered the walls; ornate lamps and sculptures sat on shiny wooden trunks; and a standing Buddha statue with a raised hand faced me from an altar-like shelf.

'Lola,' my mother said.

'The *Buddha*?'

She laughed and pointed to a macaw on a stick in the corner of the sitting room. In all the chaos, I hadn't noticed it.

'My new adoptee,' she explained. 'Needed rescuing. I've had seven.'

'*Macaws?*'

'Rescue pets. Most have been re-homed. The dogs are leaving today, so we'll only have Lola and the cats after that.' She grinned. 'I've only been back three months. One returns from India after years and years, expecting a quiet life, and this happens. Lola, meet

Nathaniel. He'll be staying with us from now on, won't you Nathaniel?'

I nodded. At the macaw. Which felt a little odd. I didn't know much about macaws, so I decided to look up some facts when I got the chance: their diet, their wing and life span, and anything unusual about their saliva. Perhaps my mother knew a little, so I asked, 'Do macaws need—?'

'Room,' she said.

'Sor—?'

'Upstairs, second on the left. Come.'

I picked up my suitcase and followed her up the rickety staircase to a very old-fashioned room. Under the low ceiling was an armchair to the left, a wooden chest of drawers holding a jug of water to the right and in the centre, a four-poster bed covered by an embroidered bedspread. On the small bedside table was a brass lamp which wasn't gas, but it wouldn't have been out of place.

'Should have seen this room a fortnight ago,' she said, stretching her lips. 'Actually, probably better you didn't. Looking shipshape now, of course.' She glanced at me, possibly for a reaction, but I was trying my hardest not to have a meltdown. My blood fizzled uncomfortably, making my skin prickle, and my heart pumped much too fast. I squeezed the red ball repeatedly. I wanted to be in Grandma's house where my room was immaculately tidy, my timetables were pinned on the walls, and the shelves were lined with books on animals and the changing planet. Not here. In this room. With her.

Through the window, I could see a field of sheep, and further in the distance, a herd of Friesian cows.

'Bit feminine,' my mother said.

'The cows?'

'The room. Haven't decorated up here yet. This was my grandmother's room. Clara. Do you remember her?'

'The one who sailed to China and walked back?'

'Precisely. Took her seven years and she lost a leg to frostbite on the way. She left this house to my father – your Grandpa Aubrey – but when his parachute didn't open during that fateful skydive in 1998, his brother Algernon inherited it. Completely batty, Algernon was. Sewed dead creatures together and tried to bring them back to life.'

I swallowed and squeezed the ball again.

'Electrocuted himself two years ago trying to create a mouse-worm. He was childless, so once he died, the house came to Nancy and me. She and Charles have their places in Scotland and France, so when I returned from India and this was empty, I moved in. Bathroom.' She opened a door at the back. Through the small window above the bath, I could see the sea.

Memories of Grandma entered my brain like a *Loa loa*, or African eye worm, which can burrow through your skin and into your eyeball, which I tried not to think about. I closed my eyes and counted to ten in eight languages. (French, Spanish, Portuguese, Italian, German, Russian, Japanese and Hindi, in that order.) It calms me down. My housemaster lets me put my headphones on and lie my head on the desk in a quiet office, too, but I could hardly do that now. Not when she was showing me around. And besides, in this house, there was almost certainly no sensory room or calm, quiet space, like Room 6a at school.

'Why do you have that?' I asked, pointing to a red water pistol on a ledge beside the toilet.

'To . . . you know. After years in India, one realizes toilet paper is unnecessary.'

'You expect me to spray a water pistol at my—'

''Course. Best way to do it. I'm trying to buy a spray gun, like they use in Asia, but they're not easy to find in Suffolk. This is the next best thing.'

I stared at the floor, horrified. I know toilet paper isn't ideal. Since 1996, around 28 million acres of Canadian boreal forest have been cut down, mainly for pulp to make toilet paper, and I avoid the softest ones because those brands often don't use recycled materials. The Romans wiped using a sponge on a stick left in a pot of vinegar, and the Talmud suggests using a handful of gravel. But a water pistol?

I counted to *saat aath nao das* and opened my eyes.

'Everything all right?' my mother asked.

I shook my head.

She left the bathroom for the bedroom and I followed, standing near the bed awkwardly with my suitcase by my feet.

'Look,' she began, wincing, 'about the mess. I *was* hoping to have got further than this by the time you arrived. I am doing my level best to . . . organize it all.' She smiled. I didn't understand why that was funny, so I diverted my attention out of the window. Looking at the cows made me feel better. Even though they weigh nearly 700 kilos, cows are calm. They have a remarkable sense of smell, too. They can probably smell what you've had for lunch when you walk past their field, which would be awkward if you'd had burgers and a milkshake.

I wondered whether all animals had an acute sense of smell and chickens could sense if you'd recently eaten chicken. Which reminded me of the girl. Did she know that chickens were the closest living relatives to the T-rex, or that their droppings contained the highest nitrogen levels of any animal, which was why they made good fertilizer? If she didn't, I'll be happy to tell her.

My mother might like to know, too, so I said, 'Chicken fertilizer is spread on crops all over the—'

'Wardrobe.'

'Sorry?'

She pointed to my case. 'You'll no doubt want to unpack.'

'Oh. Yes.'

I took my backpack off and sat it on the bed. I unzipped it and pulled out some of my most important things, placing them on the bedside table: my book, three Papermate Inkjoy pens in purple, black and blue, two spare rubber balls of different squeezing potencies, and the letter from Grandma.

My mother looked at it and then at me. 'Come down whenever you're ready,' she said, and then paused. 'Calling me Mother might be odd after all this time so you can call me Henny if you like. Beans.'

I didn't understand. 'Call you Henny if I like beans?'

'No, no. Call me Henny if you like. Different sentence. *Beans.*' She'd been moving her hands like choppers, as if that made it clearer. 'On toast. For

47

supper. Isn't that what you eat on Thursdays?' she added. 'Nancy emailed me a list. A rather . . . specific one.'

I felt relieved. 'Yes. At six-thirty.'

'Right.' She glanced at the clock and then back at me. Her eyes stayed on me a little longer than I felt comfortable with. 'I missed beans on toast in India,' she said, moving towards the door. 'Funny the things you miss.' She smiled in slow motion, her eyes wrinkling, and closed the door. I think she was trying to tell me something but I didn't know what.

I heard her chatting to Lola as if she were a neighbour who'd stopped in for tea and a bun. It must be lovely having a friend, I thought, even if it is a macaw. Even better if they're human, especially one who carries a chicken and sings to cats.

7. IVY

I was happy my singing made Misha feel better. I went to school the next morning feeling yabba-dabadoo. Still, the impossible possible was getting closer by the minute and I was desperate to show it how at one I was with all creatures and totally on their side.

That afternoon, I had another chance.

It was summer term and roasting hot – no one was in the mood to learn anything. Our teacher was really going through it as well, what with her boyfriend running off and her mother being ill: the day before, she'd asked Gus Burnham not to add to her stress because she was *this close* to the edge. She spent the rest of the lesson deep breathing, and I sat wondering what kind of edge she was on and what that even meant, which is an interesting way to spend a science lesson.

Gus Burnham added to her stress anyway. He's the kind of boy who enjoys being nasty. He's mean to people, animals, teachers – everyone. Animals warn each other about him in nudges and noises because Gus pours boiling kettles into ants' nests, pelts rabbits with his catapult, whacks cows with sticks, and pulls the wings off butterflies and moths. I hate it. He also calls me names because I'm half Thai. And because he knows I hate that as well, he does it even more. Surely the whole point of being alive is to create a nicer planet for us all to live in?

Flies don't seem to know that either, mind you. When flies fly in rectangles around the classroom, I just scowl at them. Flies are outrageously rude. Maybe because their lives aren't very long and they're not very exciting unless you're massively into poo. But when a wasp wafts right over your head in the middle of Literacy, you can't just sit there and wait for the worst to happen. Well, *you* might be able to, but I can't.

Wasps can be laid back and drifty and all, but you do *not* want to mess with them when they're drunk. They suck on fermented fruit that goes straight to their heads, making them act like idiots, fly in zigzags and pass out (a bit like drunk humans). 'Least they don't talk drivel, get aggressive or lock you in your room, like my real dad used to do. Butterflies get drunk too, and you don't even want to know about moose and fruit flies – they go looking for *their* boozy fruit. Tut. Party heads.

Fun fact: all drone wasps are called John. Every single one in Britain (I don't know about the wasps overseas). It makes it extremely easy to remember their names, but you should hear them leaving the hive in the morning. They're like, 'Morning, John,' 'Morning, John.' 'All right, John?' 'All good thanks, John.' 'Hi, John, John and John. I'm meeting up with John and John later – wanna come along?'

I'm telling you, it's nuts.

So one itty-bitty John flies into our classroom, and in zero seconds flat my whole class jumps up and starts screaming. We're not allowed to do that, obviously: we're supposed to sit in our chairs even if an aeroplane falls on to the roof or a crash of rhinoceroses charges in, but this is not what happens in the real world. I love that a group of rhinos is called a crash because that makes total sense. So does a prattle of parrots and a shiver of sharks. But a *bask* of crocodiles? That's all wrong. It should be a *lurk lunge crunch* of crocodiles, or a snap *wallop* arrrgggh or something more realistic.

'Sit DOWN, Year 6!' Miss Vickery roared.

No one sat down. Perhaps the edge was coming closer towards her, just like the creature was towards me.

I usually stay well away from Gus Burnham: he's racist, he's stupid and he's trouble, and I was actively avoiding trouble, but when trouble jumps on a chair and tries to whack a poor, innocent wasp with a pencil case – well, I'm sorry but that's a different story.

So I jumped out of my chair too – not because I was scared, but because John was in danger. This was my chance. I could save a helpless creature in peril and prove my at-one-with-the-animal-kingdom skills to the impossible possible that was heading my way.

'Leave him alone!' I roared. 'DON'T KILL HIM! I'll tell him to go out!' Obviously, I shouldn't have said that with my mouth, but it just whooshed right out and by then it was too late.

'HAHAHA! Ivy can talk to *wasps*!' Gus yelled, but no one heard him because twenty-nine gigantic humans were freaking out about a wasp one centimetre long. That's shocking, you have to admit. I was embarrassed for my species, and not for the first time. Half the kids were swaying out of John's way like they were magnetically repelled by him, and the other half were trying to bash him. Miss Vickery batted a grammar book at him, which was useless because wasps love grammar, and half the time they only sting people because they're not speaking properly. Actually, that's not true, but imagine if it was, and whenever someone said, 'I want one of them biscuits,' instead of 'I want one of *those* biscuits,' a wasp would shake its little pernickety head with disappointment and fly down to go ZZZZTTTTT.

I had to do something. And quick.

John sat on the Perspex box around the long fluorescent light, saying SCARED SCARED SCARED. I knew this was going to end badly, so I pushed past Jemima, Dan and Alice and opened all the windows as wide as I could. I cried, *John, go!* (but in my head because people look at your weirdly when you call wasps 'John'. I know this from experience). *Now, please – none of that laid-back drifty stuff, if you don't mind!*

I sent him mental pictures of the open windows and the freedom outside, far away from shrieking, violent children. Last thing I wanted was for him to be smacked with a grammar book and die after his heroic efforts to save the English language from ruin.

Then . . . BAM.

Gus whacked John against the windowsill with a

pencil case. All that was left of him was a black and yellow smear.

'Noooooooooooo!' I screamed. Through my burning eyes, I could see Gus Burnham sniggering.

'Year 6, for goodness' sake – it was just a wasp!' Miss Vickery shouted, even though she'd been terrified too, I could tell. 'Sit down, all of you! Ivy, that includes you.'

But I couldn't. I stood beside John, scratching my arm hard, my twisted face a splotch of snot and tears. The rest of the class was laughing. Gus nudged Adrian. 'Hear that, Ades? Ivy TOLD the wasp to go out.'

'Talk to the animals, can you, Ivy *Dolittle*?' Adrian yelled.

Of course I can. Not that it's any of his business.

'Wasps have just as much right to be alive as we do!' I yelled. 'So the next time a wasp is near your apple juice and you trap it inside and drown it, you might want to remember that!'

'IVY!' Miss Vickery snapped. 'Enough!'

I sat down. Miss Vickery still sent me to the Head, though, and that was bad bad bad. Not as bad as failing to save John's life, but then nothing's as bad as seeing an innocent creature suffer or die because of stupid human beings, especially when you could have saved its life if you'd tried just a tiny bit harder. I had no idea how I'd ever face wasps again. And now the impossible possible wouldn't trust me one tiny bit.

8. NATHANIEL

I trusted Grandma: if she told me to come to this chaotic house, there was a good reason for it.

I just wish I knew what it was.

I sat on the bed, picked up her letter and swallowed hard. I took it out of the envelope, gazed despondently at her neat handwriting and started reading.

Darling Nathaniel,

You have brought me joy since the day you were born, and I have enjoyed every moment I have spent in your company. I thought we had decades ahead to travel, live and learn together, but today I understand that my headaches are not merely eye strain. What I want to tell you must now be written rather than said. We anthropologists rely on studies: we learn early

*on that without written records, the way people
lived, and the joys and disasters they faced in
their lifetimes are lost for ever when they go.
With that in mind, these are just some of the
things I want to share with you, along with
important information I feel you should know.*

*I will start, and hope I will have time to
complete this.*

I looked up, blinking away the tears welling in my
eyes. I could hear her voice as if she were in the room
with me. I missed her so much.

A Holstein-Friesian mooed, breaking me from my
daydream.

I read until the end, and then read it again. As well
as writing that something was here for me, Grandma
said something else surprising – that my mother had
taken something from Mexico.

I looked around the room, then recalled the messy
house. There were so many objects here. How would
I know which one she meant? And what could my
mother have taken from Mexico that had bothered
Grandma so much?

Half an hour later, I went downstairs.

My mother was unpacking a wooden crate. I squinted, trying to determine what was in it.

'Juice,' my mother said, her head listing to the left.

'In there?'

'On the table.' She pointed to what looked like apple juice sitting in a short, thick glass tumbler on the table.

'Is it—?'

'Not from concentrate,' my mother said before I could finish my question. 'Nancy's list of what you eat and what you don't is quite extensive. I'm not sure I've got it all yet, but we can work on it.' She smiled, pulled out a dusty wooden duck and wiped it with her sleeve.

Hesitantly, I drank, wondering why 'work on it' seemed like a good thing to her.

'By the way,' she said, walking towards the dresser, 'I have similar eccentricities.' She searched for something in one of its cluttered drawers. 'I never eat anything yellow, for instance. Haven't since I was eight and vomited after too much tinned pineapple.'

I grimaced. I may like mucus but I certainly do not like vomit. Even the word is nauseating.

Untidiness surrounded me: a slapdash stack of dirty dishes sat in the sink, laundry lay in crumpled hillocks on the floor, a scattered splay of books, plastic boxes, elastic bands, batteries, hand creams, light bulbs, notebooks, electrical adaptors and skitter-scatter debris covered the table. Panicking, I counted to ten in eight languages, but I needed to learn eight more to deal with my mother's house, including Sanskrit, Classical Greek and Biblical Hebrew.

She continued rummaging in the drawer, making scratchy, jangly noises that jarred in my ears and my brain. I sat rigid, my eyes fixed compulsively on my plate to lessen the panic, and squeezed the red rubber ball in my pocket.

'Where is it . . . ? It was . . . in . . .' She opened another drawer. 'Here!' she cried, holding up a small rectangle of plastic. 'Not much to do in the evenings except read and play cards.' She closed the drawer and added, 'Wendy.'

'I don't know that game.'

My mother laughed. 'Wendy isn't a card game – she's the librarian. Library's near the fire station. Take my membership card. I'd advise going before it closes – not too busy now. You're no doubt tired after your journey, but you'll feel better about the place once you've explored a little and have some books under your arm. I know I always do. Bicycle.'

'Sorr—?'

'In the garden. Seat's low and one of the brakes is

iffy, but it works. Sweet shop.' She washed her hands over the dishes and dried them on her kaftan, then picked up her bag and started rummaging. Presumably not for a sweet shop, but I wouldn't have been surprised. 'Near the lighthouse. Buckets and spades outside, and those paper windmill things. Jars and jars of sweets inside. You buy them by weight, you see: a half-pound, a quarter. Quarter's plenty. Hand.'

She held out a hovering fist, so I placed my palm beneath it and she dropped three pound coins on to it. 'Is that enough?' she asked. 'I haven't the faintest idea how much sweets cost these days. A bag cost a few pennies when I was young.'

'Yes. Thank you,' I said. She smiled and lifted her arms out as if she wanted to embrace me, so I stood back in case she tried. 'Grandma said you did awful things when you were young,' I said. 'And one thing in particular was unforgivable.'

My mother lowered her arms. 'Direct, aren't you? I rather like it. Well, she was hardly perfect herself,' she said with a sad smile. 'We didn't see eye to eye. Very different people.'

I thought of Grandma's letter and said, 'She wrote that you took something. From Mexico. What was it?'

There was a moment's silence as she tilted her head and looked at me in a way I couldn't read. 'She didn't tell you?'

'No. She only said that she was furious because she thought you did it on purpose.'

'She did think that. In her eyes, it was the last straw.'

'That's why you stopped talking to each other, wasn't it?'

My mother gazed out of the window and said quietly, 'One reason. There were others.' She paused and added, 'She also wrote me a letter. You know, when she was in hospital. She forgave me, and she apologized.'

'I want to know what happened. With you and her, and me. I don't like mysteries.'

My mother faced me and sighed. 'Nathaniel, extended heatwaves like these are marvellously rare, the sea is bluer than I've seen it in a long while and we're spending our first summer together. I think those things are worth celebrating, don't you?'

I didn't answer. I frowned and blinked, and felt a plethora of strange sensations, from suspicion to confusion to a trickle of sweat running down my back to a scratching dog landing inelegantly on my right foot. Why weren't adults honest and straightforward?

'Now,' she went on. 'I picked you up a small map but it's easy enough to find your bearings. Not many children around yet – only the independent schools have broken up. I suggest cycling around so you get a feel of the place. Now, Lola, we have LOTS to do today,' she added, turning to her macaw.

I felt a pang of envy. Lola seemed to understand her better than I did. But it felt wrong, being jealous of a bird.

I drank the juice, put the library card in my pocket and zipped my jacket up.

'Really? Anorak?' She fanned her face with her hand.

I always wore something over my T-shirt, so it felt wrong to go out without it on. I was conflicted, though. I didn't like being hot but the anorak had . . . 'Pockets,' I said, deciding. 'Zips.'

She nodded, dubiously. 'I do love pockets. Tend to lose everything. Now where did I put my . . . ?' She walked off, mumbling.

Why did she talk so oddly? And why did people lose things? I never lost *anything*. I was extremely careful with my belongings, and very organized. Both of those aspects of her character made me feel extremely concerned.

I tried the bike out. The seat *was* low and one brake *was* iffy, but the other one worked and I could stop easily enough. I wheeled it out of the gate. As I cycled towards the library, my stomach clenched. What was my mother hiding? Why had she and Aunt Nancy not wanted me to read my letter?

I hadn't gone far when I saw her again. Not my mother, the girl. She was wearing yellow shorts, and below her dark legs, her white trainers were caked in dried mud. She wore an orange baseball hat and she was crouching with her chicken beside a basset hound, stroking it and shaking her head.

When they're stroked, dogs receive five times more oxytocin, also known as the 'love hormone', than cats do. I don't know how much humans receive, but I'm not the best person to test that on because I don't like being touched. The dog seemed to like it, though. The cantankerous owner wasn't so keen: he was pulling on its lead.

I devised a plan. I'd tell the girl a fact or two about basset hounds, and she'd want to be my friend.

So I got off my bike and waited.

9. IVY

Mr Galloway wouldn't wait. He kept pulling Clyde away when I tried to stroke him. Honestly, *I* was the one who was in a rush. *Some* of us have school till the end of July (unlike some of the kids up here on holiday) so every second of our free time is precious. Dogs don't have that problem. Lucky them.

Still, their lives aren't perfect. Dogs think humans are boring, which they are. I know this because dogs tell me.

I know you don't believe me. No one believes me. But it's true.

Poor Clyde. He's brown, black and white, with floppy ears and short legs, and he doesn't like his ploddy walk. Going the same way every day is spectacularly boring for a dog. It's boring for a human as well, but humans have very limited imaginations. You need a decent variety of smells as you go about your day. It's basic stuff.

The streets near the Sole Bay Inn don't change much from one day to the next, and the smells he gets to smell (Clyde, not Mr Galloway – well, him too, actually) are pretty much the same day in, day out. They don't go to the beach, where there are enough smells to make Clyde's nose explode, or down the high street (ditto) or to the harbour (fishy smells, mainly). They don't even go through the churchyard because Mr Galloway doesn't want Clyde to pee on the gravestones.

I listened sympathetically to Clyde's grumbling, but I had a feeling something else was wrong too. He hung his head. He felt sad, he said, because Spike, Mr Galloway's old Cocker Spaniel, had died the month before, and since then, Mr Galloway had become distant and cold. Clyde was worried that he didn't love him any more.

Obviously, I was avoiding trouble, but how could I let that carry on? Standing up for animals was my new mission. No animal I knew was going to suffer or die from now on. Not if I could help it.

'Mr Galloway,' I said, looking up at his crumpled, stubbly face, 'Clyde's tired of the same old sniffs. Could you take him a different rou—'

'Not this again,' Mr Galloway said, tugging

Clyde's lead.

'But Mr Galloway, he's—'

'He's what? What you gonna tell me today? Clyde wants to watch *Hotel for Dogs* tonight? Clyde's dream is to be a dog detective? I've heard it all. C'mon, Clyde.'

'Please.' I stood up. 'Clyde thinks you don't love him any more because you don't stroke—'

'Don't stick your nose where it don't belong,' Mr Galloway growled.

'But—'

'Leave it out, will you?' he said, and he walked off.

'You won't phone home about this, will you?' I cried (politely) as he walked away.

'Oh, I'm phoning.'

'I won't mention *Hotel for Dogs* ever again!'

'Fine,' he replied.

Clyde groaned, and so did Dot. My heart went *creeeaaaak* watching Clyde plodding around the corner, his brown-and-white nose searching for a new and exciting aroma. I'd let him down. He wasn't dead – which was excellent, obviously – but he wasn't happy, either.

If I was a professional, I thought, Mr Galloway would listen to me.

That's when I saw him. The boy from the taxi. I

hadn't seen him around town before, so I knew he was a tourist. He was about my age and he was standing beside his bike wearing a bright green anorak in the boiling heat. I don't like humans generally, and I definitely don't like boys. They have only ever been mean to me and to animals, and I learnt a long time ago to avoid them.

He was still standing there like the most awkward person in the universe, looking at me without any realization that it was actually quite rude to stand and stare at someone, so I said, 'Yes? Do you have a problem?'

'Dogs can smell what time of day it is,' he said.

'What?'

'Basset hounds have 220 million smell receptors. The collective noun could be an *investigation* of hounds. Their long ears waft the scent towards their noses, and the loose skin around their face helps trap the smell.'

'STOP!' I snapped, walking away.

'Stop what?' he asked.

'YOU'RE MAKING IT WORSE!'

'Making what worse?'

'*CLYDE!* His talents are wasted!'

'Yes, they are.' He paused and frowned. 'I do have a problem, actually.'

Was this kid for real? 'It was rhe-tor-i-cal,' I replied. 'Do you know what that means? Don't answer – that was rhetorical too. Why are you *eavesdropping*?'

He hesitated. 'Is that rhetorical?'

'Funny.' I folded my arms. 'Very funny.'

'I wasn't intending to be funny,' he said with a serious face. 'I don't understand jokes so I don't make any.'

'Weird.' I glowered. If I'd known he'd be so hugely relevant to *the thing I felt coming* and the impossible possible happening a week later on the beach (and therefore to my life in general from that day on), I wouldn't have been so snippy with him. I'll get back to the impossible possible later, because that's the most important part of this story (not that you'd know it), but you might want to picture what he looks like. It's relevant 100%. (Well, maybe 54% but that's more than 50% so it's still more relevant than irrelevant.)

He had longish brown hair that rose in a wave from his forehead and then flopped to his eyes and tickled his ears, dark grey rectangular glasses and bright blue eyes. He scrunched his nose up a lot to keep his glasses from sliding down, or maybe he just scrunched his nose a lot. He was wearing long beige shorts – and a bright green anorak, in a zillion degrees' heat.

He might sound OK to you, but as I might have mentioned, I don't like humans much. Especially boys. I don't trust them one bit. They're com-plic-ated. With animals you know where you are. When they're happy, they roll around in the mud, purr or suck on a flower stem, and when they're unhappy, they roar, sting or charge. If they're not sure, they'll wait until they are sure, and *then* they'll roar, sting or charge. But 'least they're straightforward.

I turned and walked away. I didn't have time for this.

'I saw you,' he said, pushing his bike and following me. 'With your chicken.'

It was a bit rude to ignore him, even though I wanted to, so I mumbled, 'That's nice,' and carried on walking. The sky was looking a little weak. It needed some applause, but I wasn't going to do it with the boy standing there. Wheeling gulls twirled above my head. They're so nosy, I swear. *Yaaaaaaaaaa-rrrrrrrrrrrkkkk!* one of them cried.

'Hey!' I yelled, slamming my hands on my hips and looking up. 'Stop that!' Sometimes seagulls sound like monkeys, sometimes they screech long and hard like they've just seen a member of a boy band walking down the street, and sometimes they sound like bad opera. This was a boy band screech. She did it to tell all the others that something juicy was going on, but this wasn't anyone else's business. Especially not a bunch of gossipy seagulls.

'Gulls are crafty,' he said. (I'd forgotten for a second that he was there.) 'They trick earthworms into thinking it's raining.'

I pretending I wasn't listening, but what he was saying was a tiny bit interesting.

'Worms breathe through their skin, so to move overland, their skin needs to stay wet for the oxygen to pass through. Gulls stand in a group and stamp their feet to make patting noises on the ground. The worms hear the pitter-patter, come to the surface thinking it's raining, and *shlluuuppp*, they get sucked up like spaghetti.'

Dot said, *WHAAAAT?* (in chicken language). I frowned at her. I wanted to ask him how the seagulls decided which one got to eat the worm, but that would mean starting a conversation. With a boy. Not going to happen.

I gave the gull a dirty look for making a boy have something to say to me. And then I felt it. The echo and hum of deep open emptiness. The inner push to keep going. The flap and lap. The endless blues dotted with sprinkles of sunlight.

I gasped. 'I don't have time for this,' I said, walking

on. 'It's coming. I can feel it. It's BIG and it needs my help. OMG. I keep messing up. I have to fix that. I have to … excuse me.'

And I ran off.

10. NATHANIEL

She seemed very off with me, and ran away suddenly, pushing her hair away from her face in an angry, panicky manner. I wasn't sure why. I may know lots about animal saliva but I know nothing about girls: my only cousin is thirty-two, lives in Sweden and designs bras for a living. I go to an all-boys' school, and I don't have any friends outside school, especially not girls.

What could she feel coming? Was it an animal? Could I help? Under her long black hair, she had RESCIUER written across the back of her bright pink T-shirt in black felt-tip pen.

I cycled after her and said, 'Rescuer doesn't have an I.'

She ignored me and her run slowed to a jog. She seemed to like animals too, and someone like that would be a perfect friend. 'The only thing that remotely excites basset hounds,' I said to the back of her head as she jogged, 'is a decent scent trail. They're skilled at detecting odours and flushing game out of holes. By "game" I mean rabbits, hares, ducks, geese and pheasants, and by "flushing" I mean getting them out quickly, like the toilet thing.'

The chicken was bouncing on her hip. It didn't look very comfortable for either of them.

She ignored me so I stopped cycling. 'You can feel what coming?' I called after her, but she didn't reply.

I didn't follow. She clearly didn't want to be my friend, so I turned my bike towards the library, feeling very glum.

Mr Galloway walked past with his dog. 'Don't mind her,' he said. 'She thinks they talk to her.'

'She thinks *who* talks to her?' I asked. But he carried on walking, with Clyde lumbering behind as if all the world's problems rested on his short little legs.

The library wasn't difficult to find. I thought maybe the girl had something to do with the chicken droppings on the low wall outside, but chickens and libraries aren't logical. I locked my bike, glanced again at the wall and went inside.

It was hot in there, but I felt immediately comfortable. Libraries are one of my favourite places in the world. Especially when there are no people in them. This one was empty except for the librarian.

'Let me guess,' she said, looking up. She had short grey hair, large red-framed glasses and a mole on her left cheek. 'Lady Henrietta's son?'

I fixed my eyes on the signs behind her. Looking directly at people makes me feel extremely uncomfortable. 'Yes.'

'She mentioned you'd come in. Looking for anything in particular?'

'Books on climate change, animals and mucus,' I said. 'I'll see what you have.'

She raised her eyebrows. 'Be my guest,' and returned to her computer screen. I didn't understand that comment – this wasn't really a host/guest situation – but I thought it best not to ask. I directed myself to the 8-12s section because I'm still twelve. When I turned thirteen, I'd be able to read books in the teen section, but that was three months away.

I picked up a book called *The World's Strangest Creatures*, then, although I'm not an adult, I checked the adult non-fiction section for any books on the environment. Grandma said I was allowed to because the books aren't about romance and kissing. Those books disturb me because they involve people touching and mixing their saliva. I'm not sure I'll want to read those even when I'm older.

I was reaching for *The Weather Makers* when the library door crashed open and there she was. The girl.

Wendy stood up. 'Where's that chicke—'

'Dot's outside,' the girl said, striding in. 'Don't worry, I won't bring her in. Even though this is only, like, her favourite place in the whole entire universe.'

'Better not, either,' Wendy replied, fanning her face with a pamphlet. 'And you're cleaning that wall today, young lady – it's a disgrace. The sun is baking those droppings on hard.'

I hid behind a bookshelf. So the chicken droppings on the wall *were* because of her! But why bring a chicken to the library? I stood still, peered through a gap, and listened.

'Wendy,' the girl said, 'I need a book on being an undercover animal warrior.'

'What in heaven's name is an undercover animal warrior? Do you mean someone who hunts them with spears?'

The girl gasped. 'Not that kind of warrior! I mean a *protector*. You know, so when they have problems you help them and fight for them, but without getting in trouble.'

She did love animals! I was right!

I couldn't read Wendy's face, but I saw it contort. 'Is this for your chicken or for you?' she asked.

'For me. I'll get books for Dot in a minute.'

Wendy sighed. 'Books on animal warriors . . . ? I don't think books like that even exist.'

The girl threw her arms in the air. 'Ridiculous. No one ever writes books you actually *need*! When I grow up, I'm going to write books that are useful. And save animals from boredom and sufferi—'

I dropped the book I'd been holding and it bounced on the carpet.

Footsteps marched towards me and I froze.

II. IVY

He stood there like an awkward frozen wildebeest, only with glasses and an anorak.

'You! Eavesdropper!' I snapped. 'Eavesdropping again, are we?' He wouldn't look me in the eye, which is just plain rude. I hadn't forgiven him for making me feel even worse about Clyde, and now this. 'I'm telling you, London Boy, if you're anything like Gus, you'll have me to deal with.'

He kept his eyes on the floor. 'London Boy?'

'Yes. London Boy. And that book,' I added, nodding at the one he'd dropped, 'doesn't tell you if they like poetry.'

'*Poetry?*'

'Are you a parrot? Yes, poetry. Do you know what poetry is or do you not have poems in London?'

'Of course we have poems in London,' he said, his

eyes still fixed on the book on the floor.

'Good. I should hope so.' I turned around, grabbed three picture books from the central bins, and said to Wendy, 'These, please. And I would really appreciate it if you didn't tell Jeremy what kind of books I've been asking for.'

'In trouble again, are we?' Wendy asked, scanning the barcodes.

Oh, she would have LOVED that. ''Course not,' I replied. Even though I was always in a bit of trouble. It seemed to follow me like a lost puppy.

Baaak. Dot's protest floated in through the open window. She was impatient for her story. Stories can do that to you. If you don't hear enough of them, you start clucking noisily. I know *I* do.

The boy was still standing by the bookshelves like I was going to eat him or something. He hadn't even picked the book up yet. I was about to say something but then Wendy yelped. I turned my head and saw her waving her pamphlet, boss-eyed. I thought she'd gone momentarily mad but then I saw it. A wasp. Flying towards her desk. Before I knew it, she'd pulled open the desk drawer, snatched a can of aerosol deodorant and whipped off the lid.

No! No no no no no no no.

I flung Dot's story books on the floor and darted

towards the wasp.

'*John!*' I shrieked (not even in my head). '*OUT! QUICK! Before*—'

I didn't get to finish my sentence, but John knew what I meant. He swerved and ducked, fear ripping through his whole little body. Wendy lunged at him, a crazed look on her face, the can aimed straight at him, her finger over the trigger.

NO!

London Boy leapt out from behind the shelves and stood pole-straight in front of the aerosol, holding his hand in front of the can like some kind of anti-aerosol action hero.

'Don't kill it,' he said, firmly to Wendy. 'Wasps are essential. They prey on almost every pest insect on Earth. Farmers use them to protect their crops, and we need crops or we'll all die of starvation.'

The aerosol remained in place and Wendy yelled, 'Get it out, then!'

'I'll do it!' I cried, remembering suddenly that I existed as well. I showed John the open door, but he was terrified, and when you're scared you panic, so I wafted my arms to direct him out.

Thankfully, he got the message.

'Thank you zzzzo mucchhzzzzz,' he whimpered as he hummed through the doorway.

I turned around with a frown.

*What . . . just happened? Did that boy just . . . **defend** that wasp?*

12. NATHANIEL

The wasp survived, which was very pleasing, thanks to my usual defence and some odd behaviour from the girl. What was less pleasing was that the girl was staring at me with her mouth open. *She* was the one who had talked to the wasp and called it 'John'. After a minute, she shook her head, gathered her books from the floor and walked outside.

Wendy put the aerosol down. 'I just zap them,' she said, slotting the lid back on the can, 'usually.'

She clearly didn't realize the importance of wasps. Someone needed to tell her, and that someone had to be me. 'The volume of food needed to feed the world in the next forty years is more than we've harvested in the rest of human history,' I said. 'Wasps are as ecologically essential as bees for our global food security and health.'

Wendy flared her nostrils and looked at the ceiling. 'Oh, dear God, not another one.'

I thought it was an odd time for her to pray, but I waited until she'd finished, then carried on. 'A small wasp colony eats up to three thousand flies, mosquitoes and spiders each day, and kills insects that carry human diseases.'

'Doesn't mean I want them in my library, though,' she said. 'Does it? Not wasps and not chickens, thank you.' She flapped her face and glanced at the door. 'Speaking of which, you've got five minutes of peace before she finishes reading her chicken those stories and comes back in.'

She shut the aerosol in her drawer. I wanted to tell her that aerosols contain volatile organic compounds (VOCs), which contribute to ground-level ozone and asthma-inducing smog. Nail polish, perfume, mouthwash and hairsprays also emit VOCs. This seemed especially important to mention because Wendy had burgundy nails, smelt of perfume and probably used hairspray, as her hair stood upright and didn't move. But I would need to use her library to research further, and I wanted her to let me in, so instead I asked, 'Who is she? Why does she read stories to a chicken?'

'Her?' The librarian rolled her eyes. 'Ivy Pink Floyd. Bane of my life.' She looked at the door and mouthed, '*Difficult past.*' Then in a normal voice, she pointed to the book that was still on the floor and added, 'Taking that out?'

I retrieved the book. 'Yes, please. *Ivy Pink Floyd?*'

She scanned it, squinting at the door. 'Floyd's her surname. Her parents must have been fans of the band. Mind you, her mother was from Asia and I'm not sure how big Pink Floyd were out there. Come back whenever you like, but do me a favour. Leave your pets at home.'

'I don't own any pets.'

She handed me the book. 'Good.'

'My mother does, but I won't bring them in here. If I had a choice, I'd have a yeti crab, a sucker-footed bat or an axolotl.' I moved towards the door. I could have stayed inside until Ivy Pink Floyd left, but there was something interesting about a girl with a difficult past reading stories to a chicken.

'. . . *then over the hill marched the mouse to his house, and he*—' She stopped reading as I walked out. I could feel her eyes on me.

Buck buck buck buck buck buck, squawked her hen. She was walking around on the grass near Ivy's feet.

'Sorry,' Ivy said. '. . . *and he wanted to play but the cow said, "No way," so he curled in the hay for the rest of the day. The End.*'

Buck buck buck.

'Like that one, Dot?'

Baaaak.

'Me too. OK, enough. I know you can't tell a hen who likes stories only two of them because she'll squawk at you for a week, but I've got stuff to do.'

I gave my blue rubber ball a squeeze and placed the book in my bike basket.

Buck buck buck buck.

'I *said* no more,' Ivy said, but then she picked up a different book. 'Fine. One more, then. *A Dragon in a Wagon*, by Lynley Dodd. Like this one, don't you? Top book, this. But no more after this. I'm on a mission. No more wasp and hamster deaths.'

Hamster deaths?

This was my chance.

'Hamsters have scent glands on their hips that help them navigate,' I began. 'They're more prominent in males. They lick the fur near the glands to form damp spots, then drag themselves along objects. It marks their territory but also helps them find their way home. They can't see very well, you see.'

She closed the book and scowled at me.

'Golden hamsters are known as "Mister Saddlebags" in Arabic because of the way they stuff their cheeks. Sadly, their numbers are declining in the wild. They're now classified as "vulnerable", which means they're in danger of becoming extinc—'

'NOOOOOOO!' she howled, and covered her face with her hands. I think she was crying.

'OK,' I said, feeling extremely awkward. I was aware it wasn't OK to be so upset, but I'd never had that reaction from telling animal facts before and I didn't know what to do. Mortified, I found the bicycle pedal with my foot and tried to make her feel better. 'If you really want to help animals,' I said, 'avoid wearing brightly coloured T-shirts and jeans. The dyes they use are toxic and contaminate rivers and lakes.'

She wailed, 'The problem with being eleven is that no one takes you seriously. The world is so big and the problems are so vast and it's all happening too quickly!'

'Exactly. But we could set up some kind of action agency,' I suggested. 'If we were friends.'

She stopped wailing and wiped her eyes. 'Action agency?' She paused. 'Not a bad idea but it won't work. When you're an eleven-year-old girl who communicates with animals, no one takes you seriously times a hundred.'

'Communicates with animals?'

'URGH! Even you don't believe me!' She shot up and marched back in with her book, leaving me standing outside in the heat with Dot pecking at the grass and me wondering what in the world Ivy Pink Floyd was talking about.

13. IVY

The world was falling apart around my ears. I had no time to talk to weird boys. I took the book back in and handed it to Wendy. As I stood at her desk, I looked down at my clothes. *Toxic dyes?* Wait – there were *clothes* that were animal-friendly? Should I only wear white? Walk around *naked*?

And *action agency*? Now, that was a brilliant idea.

'Wendy,' I said, 'Emergency.'

'Lord above, what now?'

'I need books on animal action agencies.'

'I should have taken that job at the dentist,' Wendy muttered to herself. 'What's an anim— do you mean like the RSPCA?'

'What? No. Oh, *aaaagency*. No, no, not that kind. I mean like a detective agency but, you know, for animals. So they can come to you with their problems and you can help them fight back. Against humans.'

Wendy sighed. 'I've got something for you.' She went into the back and came out with a bucket of water, a brush and some disinfectant.

'This is not the best time for me to clean the wall,' I said, blinking hard so she'd understand I was upset.

'Do it. Now. Or no more books.'

'Hrrrgghh.'

Quickly as I could, I scrubbed the wall, then grabbed Dot and ran home.

On the way back, I told Dot about being sent to the Head that day. She loves hearing about my dramas at school, especially the ones involving animals. 'After John got splatted, I kept my head down,' I told Dot, 'hoping Miss Vickery would forget about it. But then a dog barked outside and Gus shouted, "Ivy, what's it *saying?*"

Bukbukbukbukaaak, said Dot.

''Course I did. I knew exactly what it was saying. It was saying I DON'T LIKE YOU I DON'T LIKE YOU I DON'T LIKE YOU. I didn't know who it was talking to because we're not allowed to look out of the window during History, but it was exactly how I felt about Gus. That's not *always* what dogs say when they bark – you know that, right, Dot? Sometimes they're like, HEY YOU! HEY! HEY! GET AWAY FROM MY HOUSE! or WOAH JEEZ YOU

SCARED THE LIVING DAYLIGHTS OUT OF ME or CAT CAT LOOK THERE'S A CAT QUICK COME SEE THE CAT WHY AM I THE ONLY ONE WHO'S INTERESTED IN THIS CAT?'

Bukbukbukbukbuk.

'I *am* getting on with it. So Percy was like, "Ignore him, Ivy," which was nice of her and everything, but then Miss Vickery said, "Ivy, the Head wants to see you," and pointed to the door.'

Baaaaaaakkkkk.

'Exactly. Miss Stansfield's like a grizzly bear with toothache. "Would you like to explain what happened?" she asked. When humans ask you that, Dot, the answer is always *No, thank you*, but you can never say that. I don't know why they bother asking. It's called a rhetorical question, which is a question that floats around in the air with its little question-marky-hook looking desperately for something or someone to hook on to. It's like a ghost question that was once alive and is now trapped in punctuation limbo. Why on earth would a normal, rational human being ask a question they didn't want an answer to?'

I paused and added, 'Oh. I just did it myself. Haha.'

Baaaaakbakbakbak.

'OK, keep your feathers on – I'm getting there. So

in my politest voice, I said, "Miss Stansfield, it is shocking when humans behave like that." You know what she said? She said, "Miss Vickery is going through a difficult time, Ivy, and your behaviour is causing her additional stress."

'"That poor wasp *died*!" I pointed out.

'She said, "Are you listening to me, Ivy?"

'Honesty is always the best policy, so I admitted that I wasn't. So she sighed and said, "Take this letter home, and you can forget about accidentally losing it on the way because I'll phone your foster parents later to check." Which isn't fair – I really did lose it last time. I was leaning over the river to help an eel and it fell in.'

Baaakbakbakbak.

'Right. I *told her* I feel more frog and dog than girl, but she rubbed her eyes and said she had emails to write.'

Baaaakk.

'Actually, she's OK for a human, but I much prefer creatures. Even wasps. Although I'm not that keen on the drunk ones.'

Baaakbakbakbakbak.

Dot liked my story, but I was nervous. I was supposed to be staying out of trouble and *being there* for the huge thing on its way – and now this.

When we got home, I took Dot out to the garden. She'd had quite enough excitement for one day. Then I went upstairs to change.

The wardrobe in the guest room is full of weird things: single shoes, Aisling's old handbags, a compass that doesn't face north, a map of the Gobi Desert, a book called *The Wonders of Bicarbonate of Soda* and some of Daddy Jeremy's old work shirts. He was an architect before he retired. He's very tall so the shirts are huge, but they're white, and I was recycling, which had to be good.

I put one on, changed my jeans shorts for grey soft ones and dug my red wellies out from under my bed. I wasn't sure about the wellies. Weren't they made of plastic? Wasn't plastic bad?

I couldn't look it up because we don't own mobile phones or laptops. Jeremy and Aisling don't use them and they don't want me to, either.

You might be wondering how I entertain myself with no screens. You might not because you might not care about screenless people like me – or be interested in my life at all – and that's OK. If you're not on the endangered species list, I'm not massively interested in yours, either. But if that's the case, you're probably also the kind of person who also doesn't believe in communication with animals, and that's a real shame. The truth is, I believe this old-fashioned life helps with my animal intuition: there's no interference from technology or radio waves, and I have no distractions, so I can tune in to animals and become, you know, one. Just don't ever ask me if I've watched a boxette on Nightflix or to follow you on InstaChat, because I won't know what you mean.

I took a deep breath and went downstairs to face the music. (I don't know why it's called that when music is a nice, happy thing and this wasn't going to be a nice, happy thing at all. I'd change it to 'face the huge hairy monster' or 'face the dreaded History homework', but that's just me.)

I had failed animals again and again, and that was bad. But now I'd failed Jeremy and Aisling, too, and that was extra bad. I could lose my home, and the impossible possible might go elsewhere instead, and both of those things made me swallow very hard indeed.

14. NATHANIEL

I followed a swallow half the way home, but it swerved westwards over the fields, leaving me longing for wings instead of a bike.

As I cycled, I thought about Ivy. I'd tried to make friends with her. Why did it never work? Was I so incredibly horrible that no one wanted to be with me except my family, who had to?

Unfortunately I couldn't save the world on my own, and neither could Ivy. But what did she mean about communicating with animals?

Cycling around, it was easy to see why Southwold was popular. I pedalled along sunlit roads and paths, past the long, sandy coast, which was lined with colourful beach huts. A wide promenade had steps to the beach, and at the far end was an arcade and pier. Behind the seafront, a rising road turned into a cliff with a tall lighthouse, and behind that was a brewery and a high street with shops selling gourmet fudge, ornamental lighthouses and stripy clothes to people who by the looks of it already had plenty of stripy clothes. To the left were houses and churches and dunes; the rest was just cows, estuaries and reeds as far as the eye could see. At the far end, near a tall concrete water tower was a harbour where children crouched near the edge of the bank, lowering strings into the water, then shrieked as they pulled them up. Intrigued, I stood beside one family and asked what they were doing.

'Crabbing,' the girl said.

Crabbing?

Up close, I could see better. They secured bait on a round metal weight at the end of the line, lowered the line into the water and fished it out with crabs hanging off it (hence the shriek). Some crabs fell off the line on the way up, but any that didn't, they put into a bucket, repeatedly trying to count how many they had before tipping the crabs back into the water when it was time to go home.

The family seemed a little uncomfortable that I was standing so close and watching them, which made *me* feel uncomfortable, so I said, 'The largest crab in the world is the giant Japanese Spider Crab, which can measure up to thirteen feet across.'

'Wow,' the mother said. 'We wouldn't be able to fit that in our bucket, would we, Aggie?'

Aggie didn't answer.

''Course, *Homarus americanus*, the American lobster, often weighs more than twenty kilos, making it the heaviest crustacean in the world,' I added.

They looked at me oddly, so I walked over to another group. They counted how many they had – 'Twenty-seven!' – and tipped them back into the water.

'The largest crab in the world,' I told them, too, 'is the giant Japanese Spider Crab—' but they were busy packing up and walking to their car.

One thing I learnt that day was that crabs like bacon. Now that's something you don't read about in books.

By now it was supper time, and I hadn't made a friend, helped the world or found whatever it was Grandma had said was here for me.

I approached Huntington House, feeling queasy. The mess in there was overwhelming, and my mother was confusing. Not only that, her relationship with Grandma had been awful, and I didn't know why.

I passed the row of cannons on Gun Hill – another mystery – knocked on the door, and my mother answered with Lola perched on her finger.

'Hello,' I said. 'What's—?'

'A key?'

'I know what a key is,' I replied. 'What's Gun Hill?'

'But you don't have one.'

'A gun or a hill?'

'A key,' she said. 'Hand.'

I held out my hand and she dropped a key into it. 'So you don't have to knock.' She squinted at the cannons. 'Yes, Gun Hill. Hot.'

I waited but realized she was only remarking on the weather, so I zipped the key into my pocket and then took my anorak off, which I was glad about, as I'd been sweating.

My mother pointed to the beans on toast and I sat at the table. I didn't eat. I closed my eyes and counted to ten in eight languages. She waited for me to finish and then asked, with her head inclined, 'What?'

'I eat sourdough bread, medium sliced.'

'I see. Anything else?'

'Space between the slices. And the beans shouldn't spill over the crust on to the plate.'

She tapped her fingers on the table. 'I see. The bakeries are closed now. I can't . . .' She trailed off. 'So perhaps just for this evening?'

I scraped the beans off the bread, and ate those reluctantly, wondering what my mother had done that was so unforgivable and what could possibly be here for me, buried under all this chaos. There had to be clues somewhere, but where would I start looking?

After supper, the phone rang. It was Uncle Charles. My mother made stiff small talk with him for a minute or two, then gave me the handset and went into the garden.

'Using your time wisely, Nathaniel?' he asked. I wasn't sure if I was, but he didn't wait for an answer. 'I've asked Rory to collect you on the eighteenth and chaperone you to London. I'll meet you at Liverpool Street and bring you to Sussex. Nancy will be in theatre, so she'll come back once she's finished.'

Aunt Nancy was a surgeon. I liked talking to her about her work. It was always interesting to hear about internal organs and bodily liquids. Uncle Charles was an insurance broker. Talking to him was less interesting and always made me feel as though a disaster was about to happen. Speaking of which . . .

'Um,' I began. 'Could someone else—?'

'No, no. Spoken to Rory about the taxi. Won't happen again. Didn't realize he was to wait with you, you see.'

I didn't argue, but the thought of seeing Rory again was not a happy one.

'Nathaniel?' Aunt Nancy's soft voice was comforting. 'How are you? How is it with . . . Henrietta?'

Aunt Nancy didn't get on with my mother, either. They only talked when they had to. Aunt Nancy preferred to email.

'It's untidy and confusing,' I replied.

Aunt Nancy paused. 'Yes, well, that's Henrietta for you.'

'Er . . . Grandma wrote in her letter that my mother took something from Mexico.' I looked through the window. My mother was under the beech tree, grappling with an old cast-iron trellis, which she was no doubt taking to the skip in the back. Everything seemed to be going to the skip, but the house never seemed any emptier because more boxes kept appearing from the attic. 'Do you know what it was?'

After a pause, Aunt Nancy said, 'Your mother is an entity unto herself.'

'I don't know what that means.'

'It means that for most of her life, she hasn't cared about anything or anyone except herself, and we've had to pick up the pieces. She claims to have changed, but—' Aunt Nancy made an odd growly noise. 'We have guests,' she went on. 'I must see to them. Take care, now, Nathaniel. We'll see you very soon.'

And she put the phone down.

15. IVY

That evening, I felt quite down as Daddy Jeremy read the letter. Poor John. I couldn't save him and if I couldn't even save a wasp, what could I do to help the *big thing coming*?

Daddy Jeremy, Aisling and I were sitting around the table, which is where all our serious discussions take place. Not being able to save a wasp definitely deserves a serious discussion. But they were more concerned with me getting in trouble with the Head. Adult priorities are very strange.

The table always looked the same. It was round with a lace doily in the middle and a white china ornament of milkmaids on top that belonged to Aisling's mother. Twice a year, it had a cut-glass vase on it (the kind that tings when you flick it), filled with pink carnations, but only on their wedding anniversary in May and on Aisling's birthday in December.

They're very predictable, my foster parents. They're getting on a bit, you see (that's putting it nicely). They have grey hair and papery skin on their hands, and they enjoy doing peaceful things, like gardening while listening to Radio 4, then coming in to have a nice cup of tea and watch gardening programmes on TV. Our house is not very exciting. (That's putting it nicely, too.) They're extremely lovely, but living with them is a bit like going back a hundred years to when clocks still needed winding and a single afternoon seemed to last for three weeks.

'Hmmm,' Daddy Jeremy said, frowning. I was frowning too because my house smelt of fish. I don't eat fish. Fish are my friends and I don't eat my friends. I don't eat my enemies either, or I'd eat Gus Burnham with chips and ketchup. A tin of baked beans sat on the counter, which must have been for me, but just smelling the fish made me feel sad. 'Ivy, would you kindly elucidate?'

Even if you don't know the long words Daddy Jeremy uses, you can usually figure them out. I happen to know that 'elucidate' means to clarify or shine a light on something, because he uses that word all the time. I squeezed my bum cheeks (look, it was a high-stress situation), wondering whether the truth was a good idea. But I'm not good at lying. Especially not to him. So I came straight out with it.

'No one believes I can communicate with animals,' I said, throwing my hands in the air.

'Ah.' He peered at me over his glasses. 'This again.'

'Yes, this again! Miss Vickery doesn't believe me, Miss Stansfield doesn't believe me – no one believes me!'

Aisling pinched her lips so her mouth area looked like the Earth in a drought. Aisling is very proper. She wears a tidy string of pearls, and colour-coordinated clothes that fit her. Unlike me. She thinks I'm a bit of an embarrassment, but *I'm* not the one who covers my hair with a plastic bag when it's raining.

The grandfather clock ticked and the sound echoed off the wooden floors, like it was tutting. In a house as silent as ours, you can hear that in my room upstairs. *Tut. Tut. Tut. Naughty Ivy. Tut. Tut.*

Aisling took a breath in through her nose – I heard it whistle – and said, 'Jeremy, remember what Eileen told us?'

My toes curled. Eileen is my social worker. She tells them lots of things I don't like.

'That after a trauma, some children create a fantasy world because reality is too difficult for them to manage,' Aisling continued. 'We can't encourage her, Jeremy. Norman phoned this morning: she's been pestering him about Clyde again, and Wendy's complaining about the library wall. This can't continue.'

Jeremy's eyebrows danced like uncles at a wedding. He peered at me. 'Ivy, my dear, what was formerly an imaginative game is no longer acceptable behaviour. You are eleven now, and these stories of yours are akin to telling lies.'

That's how he speaks. He actually says 'akin'. You get used to it after a while.

I flinched. 'But . . . this isn't a *game*,' I began. Surely no one would punish me for telling the truth. It went against everything that was right and fair in the world. Where was the *justice*? 'I really *can* communicate with animals.'

His fingers made a steeple. 'They talk to you, do they?'

'Well, yes, but . . . it's more like this . . . understanding. I . . . *I* don't know . . . I can *feel* them in my head and in my insides. I sense who they are, what they need and what's bothering them. They tell me things.'

'I see.'

'It's like . . . it's like, right . . . it's like I forget everything else exists and I tune in to their souls and their minds. We have this . . . *conversation*. And it's *a-ma-zing* because we become, like, one.' I waved my hands in a

101

circle to elucidate.

Aisling blinked and cleared her throat. Jeremy continued peering at me over his glasses, his eyebrows now doing the can-can. *Tut*, went the clock. It's so judgemental. Then Jeremy looked at Aisling in *that* way. Why did no one ever believe me? Not even them, and they'd said they'd be right behind me, no matter what.

'The truth is,' I added quickly, 'anyone can do it, but most people don't know they can. People go around thinking *we're* humans,' – I slammed both hands to the left of the table top – 'and *they're* animals,' – I slammed both hands to the right – 'but they forget humans ARE animals.' I brought my hands together and rubbed them. 'It's basic stuff.'

There was a silence while I let them take that in. The kind of silence that's screaming with noise. They'd get it. They had to. A thousand interesting incidents happened in that short pause. A mouse in Russia stole some cheese from a trap without being caught. A sloth in Panama relaxed so much, he fell out of a tree. People in America held weddings for their dogs in bride and groom costumes. That kind of thing.

'You . . . believe me, don't you?' I asked, looking from Aisling's concerned face to Jeremy's confused one.

Something inside me sank like a teddy stuffed with rocks that you place in a pond to keep the fish happy (not relevant). I was used to Aisling shaking her head in exasperation at what I got up to, but not Daddy Jeremy. Aisling was kind and patient, and baked great pies, but Daddy Jeremy was the human I felt most comfortable with in the entire world. I knew that whenever it felt like I was falling down a big well, he'd be there to grip my wrist so I wouldn't slip yelling *Aaaaarrrrggggggghhh!* with a deathsplat at the end. Now he was frowning and looking disappointed too, when all I wanted was for him to smile his kind smile and put his hand on top of mine and I'd know everything would be all right. Like he did when I was five and they gave me a home and saved me.

Jeremy shifted on his chair. 'Ivy, Aisling and I can't help but wonder—'

I glanced at Aisling: how did he know if she wondered the same thing as he did? Could they communicate without speaking, like I could with animals?

'—whether Eileen is right when she says you need to be around more children your own age. Are you lonesome, Ivy? Fostering just one child can have its drawbacks . . . and you with your . . . er . . . past and so forth. Is that why you say you can . . . uhhh . . .

communicate with animals?'

My guts twisted. I started scratching my left arm hard and Jeremy put his hand over mine, making my heart fill up. 'No more of that, now, Ivy. No more scratching.'

I pushed my hands under the table and tried to stay calm. 'Daddy Jeremy,' I whispered, the blood draining from my face, 'I say I can communicate with animals because it's 100% true.'

Jeremy sighed. 'Ivy, Aisling agrees with me when I say—'

How could she possibly agree when he hadn't said it yet?

'—that this can't go on. This . . . er . . . gift of yours is best kept under wraps, at least for the time being. Until we ascertain the optimal route of action. It's causing a rumpus, you see. And we don't want one of those, now, do we?'

I shook my head. We did not. I liked being there, and they liked fostering me. So much that they'd applied for me to stay with them as my permanent home. That would mean Eileen couldn't send me to live with other foster families like she was planning to do, or put me back in the children's home where the other kids were mean to me and the concrete of the city made my chest and my eyeballs hurt, and where I hid under tables scratching my arms until the skin was raw and I wasn't allowed any pets. Not even insects. Definitely not Dot or Rufus.

'No rumpus,' I said, quietly. 'I'll keep a low profile.'

'That would be wise. And you may wish to review your level of honesty, hmm?'

My throat clenched. 'But I *am* being honest.'

Aisling sighed. I think she was expecting to foster a girl who'd bake with her and let her plait her hair, and instead she got one who marches around town with a hen under her arm talking to animals and bringing them home for breakfast (not relevant).

I sat feeling sorry for myself and my many rubbish failures, and panicking because the impossible possible was coming and needed me, but now I had to be very good and it was all too complicated.

Daddy Jeremy nodded to himself. 'Let's have tea, shall we?' he suggested brightly, and he got up and turned the kettle on.

16. NATHANIEL

The next morning, I was woken by the whistling of the kettle, which sounded like children screaming into my ears at close range. Noises like air conditioners, fireworks, car alarms and lawnmowers; smells like frying food, perfume and fabric softener; sensations like itchy, tight clothes (on me) and zigzagged or patterned clothes on other people make me feel I'm on a boat in a storm with twenty heavy metal bands playing at the same time and I can't find the exit and the deck's moving and my head and body are being pressed together by a machine that crushes cars.

I pulled my pillow over my head and counted to ten in eight languages until it stopped. Grandma didn't have unbearable noises like that in her house. Couldn't my mother have a silent kettle? Or not drink tea? Why did adults like tea so much? When did it stop tasting of boiled blankets and start being tasty?

The noise stopped. Noise bothers animals too. It interferes with birds' migration patterns, for one thing. The rise in global noise levels is at least partly responsible for plummeting species numbers. Planes, motorbikes, pneumatic drills, loud music, cars, whistling kettles – there were so many modern-day objects that emitted noise. Not to mention the impact of invisible things, like radiation, especially from mobile phones, and pollution.

I tried to calm my rapid breathing by standing in the bathroom and staring at the sea. It always made me feel better, even though it reminded me of Grandma. When I was six, she had given me an atlas with beautiful illustrations. The land was blank, green and empty, but the oceans were blue and teeming with sea creatures, amphibians, corals and rock pools. I loved that book most of all, and we had an entire library to choose from.

'Oceans remind us that not everything is about human beings,' Grandma used to tell me, which was strange because she was a professor of anthropology. Anthropologists study how people live, and people tend to live on the land. She loved societies, tribes and cultures – both living and long-gone – because she thought people, their roots and their stories were what made the world such a wonderful place. Her area of speciality was Central America, specifically the Seri people of Mexico, who have a close connection to the sea and believe that turtles are sacred.

Grandma and I talked about turtles often. We were a month away from travelling to Mexico to see leatherbacks, our favourites, when doctors discovered she had a brain tumour. To make up for not being able to go, she bought me posters and books on leatherbacks, and while she had chemotherapy we read books and watched programmes about them in her hospital room.

We never got to see them.

Sometimes, when I'm in bed, I imagine swimming with Grandma in a clear, green ocean full of turtles. We're together and we're happy. And we always will be.

I don't tell anyone that.

I reached for the letter. Just seeing Grandma's handwriting made my stomach tense.

She began with her time in Mexico, thirty years before, when she was a PhD student.

The Seri don't warm to outsiders – they're second only to the Apache in their ferocity as warriors – so our research group camped on the beach on a small island near Tiburon, and formed a small community with the other scientists there. It was a beautiful bay with clear water and turtles, mainly leatherbacks, swimming right front of us. What a joy it was to be there, to wake up there! It was idyllic, Nathaniel — just heavenly. I loved it.

And then, just before I left Mexico to complete my doctoral studies in England, your mother and Nancy came to visit. They were teens, and teens often do foolish things. Your mother was reckless and irresponsible at the best of times; Nancy was always more sensible, but she was easily influenced by your mother back then.

I don't know what they were thinking but your mother persuaded Nancy to take something home that they shouldn't have. When I found out, I was disgusted. Horrified. I didn't tell a soul about it: I was too afraid of getting in serious trouble just as the university was considering my research findings and my career was about to begin. And even though it came to nothing, in the end, our relationship was never the same again.

I've written your mother a letter, too. I regret spending all those years being furious with her and keeping her apart from the person she loved more than anything. Please go there in the holidays, Nathaniel, and get to know her. You need to connect with people, especially her. She is your mother, after all. And do try to make some friends. You'll be such a good one.

I lowered the letter. What had my mother taken from Mexico that was so bad that they stopped speaking? And Grandma was right. I did need a friend.

What I didn't know then was that I'd already met one, and she would enter my life like a whole colony of exploding ants.

Just as well, really. Some things are best not to know in advance.

17. IVY

Saturdays are the best days ever. It's hard to save the world when you need to go to school.

Most Saturday mornings, I go beachcombing, looking for lost things. Sometimes I do quite well. I've found a pink plastic watch, some huge white sunglasses, a stripy bikini top (age 8–9), and a big yellow flip-flop that didn't fit either of my feet. Things like that I leave on the walkway so their owners can find them the next day, but if I find money, I keep it. I often find 20ps, 50ps, sometimes pound coins. It all adds up, you know. And I'm lucky because I can go beachcombing pretty much every day, seeing as the beach is at the end of my road. Once I found a damp ten-pound note poking out of the sand (definitely the highlight of my beachcombing life). Long as no one is around, any dropped money is yours for the taking.

But that Saturday, I didn't go beachcombing. I had

more important things to do. I'd agreed to keep a low profile to avoid every possible rumpus, but the impossible possible was coming closer and closer; it needed to know I was trustworthy and that everything would be OK.

If I couldn't prove I could do this, then that made me feel like the worst animal warrior in the world.

So I woke up early and got dressed in my new animal warrior uniform: one of Daddy Jeremy's old work shirts to scoop things up, like hollow shells, careless bugs and hermit crabs that might need a change of scenery (also useful for wiping oil slicks off starfish and seagulls, except you can't expect to wear that particular shirt ever again), some shorts and my red wellies (to save drowning insects in deep water and sing to microscopic creatures in rock pools).

Then I went into the garden. Daddy Jeremy was kneeling beside a rose bush in gardening gloves. It was a hazy summer morning, the kind where pleased bees eagerly gorge themselves by nibbling on nectar, the light was a sweet, buttery yellow, like the inside of a vanilla sponge cake, and the wind was as nimble, light and flighty as butterflies in love. It would have been perfect if I hadn't recently buried an assassinated hamster, grieved for a splatted wasp, failed a depressed dog and scrubbed a poo-ey wall because Wendy cared more about a clean library than a happy hen.

'Daddy Jeremy,' I said, 'what would one need in order to set up an action agency?' (I used the word 'one' on purpose because it's a clever way of being hypothetical, which means I'm only *considering the idea, in theory*, and *not thinking of doing it myself or anything* ha ha, *'course* not. Why would *I* want to do anything radical or useful? HAHA. I'm just asking, you know, *generally*, because I'm educating myself about the ways of the world and what have you.)

Jeremy frowned. He does that a lot when he's talking to me. 'Er,' he said, inspecting the rose bush, 'I'm not entirely certain, but one assumes it would require a person – or *persons* – to run the agency, and possibly a desk and a phone.' He paused for nearly enough time for another rose to grow. A crow cawed in the old oak. A fog of midges loitered hyperactively nearby and then trembled off. A greenfly tried desperately to blend into the stem, hoping all the while that Jeremy's eyesight wasn't good enough to see it.

He'd said 'persons' instead of 'people', and I was quite sure that if I said that in school, I'd get told off. I made a mental note to ask him about it later. And he made it quite clear that 'persons' would be better than 'person', so a proper agency must need more than just me in it.

Then I felt it. The echo and hum of deep open emptiness and the inner push to keep going. The flap and lap. The endless blues dotted with sprinkles of sunlight. 'But if . . . one . . . *were* to open an agency,' I persevered, 'would . . . one's foster father help one and not get angry?'

His eyebrows did one of those Victorian dances, the kind where the partners touch hands and walk around each other in circles. Or so it seemed to me.

'Perhaps one's foster father wouldn't *help* one, but wouldn't necessarily punish one, either,' he replied. 'Depends how much . . . attention . . . it might attract. Zero is acceptable. Anything more is not.'

I nodded. 'But if it's crucially important . . .'

'Ivy,' he said gently, putting down his secateurs. 'Do you like living here?'

I blinked hard. Salty water formed a thin film over my eyes and my belly felt hurricane-y. 'Of course. It's the best thing that ever happened to me,' I whispered.

'And to us, Ivy. And to us.'

'You're the nicest humans I've ever known. And ever will know.'

Daddy Jeremy's eyes were soft and kind. 'Likewise. Which is why we can't give them even the tiniest reason to separate us. Do you see?'

I nodded. 'I do, but—'

'Besides, I doubt Rufus or Dot would manage,' Daddy Jeremy said, 'without you.' He went back to his pruning and I stood beside him, thinking.

I needed Daddy Jeremy and Aisling, and they needed me back.

I needed Rufus, and Rufus needed me too. Not to mention Dot. Who would read her stories?

And all that neediness-ness was crisscrossed like a giant cat's cradle. I didn't want to lose my foster home, my two daddies (human and dog) and my happy life – but I couldn't let creatures down, either.

I looked at Rufus and his big brown eyes sank into mine. *But the creature*, I said to Rufus. *I can't let it down. It needs me, too.*

Rufus licked my hand.

'Do one-person agencies attract any attention?' I asked Daddy Jeremy.

'Quite possibly, Ivy. Although not having an agency at all might attract zero, and that's the number we're after.'

What if I helped them quietly? I thought, encouraged by Rufus's hand-lick. *There were quiet, solo warriors, surely. I just had to work alone and attract zero attention and everything would be fine.*

'Thank you, Daddy,' I said (to my foster father, not to Rufus, although I've said it to Rufus plenty of times). I gave Daddy Jeremy a hug and he stiffened like a giant dead hamster, which I didn't want to think about. He's not the most natural hugger in the world.

After lunch, I pedalled past the lighthouse, down Chester Road and along the beachfront with an empty drinks crate over my head, an old landline telephone in my basket and a sign on a string around my neck.

Cycling like that wasn't easy, especially in wellies: I nearly knocked over a toddler who wandered in front of me and then, when I swerved to avoid a ladybird, the crate slid over my eyes, I crashed into the kerb and went flying. But I picked myself up, helped the ladybird to a nearby bush and wiped the blood off my knees with my shirt. Then I put the crate back on my head and carried on cycling until I reached the pier.

Seagulls were circling above, screeching LOOK! LOOK! LOOK AT HER! LOOK! so of course other gulls flew overhead to see what they were looking at. Yes, I must have looked hilarious with the crate balanced on my head as I zigzagged down the road, but apart from a couple of mickey-takers, the gulls were mostly cheering me on. I think they knew what I was on my way to do, even though they couldn't read the sign around my neck because they haven't mastered the alphabet yet.

I don't hold it against them. They're clever in other ways. What I personally learnt that morning was that gulls are good at making announcements, so I made a mental note of it in case I needed them later. It was reassuring, knowing the entire animal kingdom was behind me, except for a few frisky seagulls.

Through the slots in the crate I could tell what sort of day it was going to be. The tide was out, and the sea beyond the shingle was a brilliant shade of blue, not the usual cold grey mass, churning and swelling like undigested porridge in a vomity stomach. The sky was fragile, as if it really wasn't sure about itself and needed a round of applause, so when I got off my bike at the pier, I gave it one. You know, to boost its self-esteem. I'm not sure about this but I think it went a tiny bit bluer. All it needs is love, really. Like most things.

I took the crate off my head and rubbed the places where it had been pressing. Crates aren't comfortable to carry on your head, in case you wondered. This one was from the storage area at the back of the Adnams' shop. Bernard who works there said I could take it if I returned it later. He's nice: he always gives me a biscuit so I'll go away and leave him alone.

I propped my bike between Ceezruf II and 75d (strange names for beach huts if you ask me, but 75d has a sign in the window saying, 'I don't skinny dip, I chunky dunk' so I like that one).

Jellyfish were visiting, so I said hi to them, and then I felt it.

The echo and hum of deep open emptiness. The inner push to keep going. The flap and lap. The endless blues dotted with sprinkles of sunlight. And there was something else. A swell of love and heaviness, and all I could see were smooth white balls. Lots of them.

So I set off down the pier.

18. NATHANIEL

'It's not far from the pier,' my mother announced after I ate my breakfast. She had found some sourdough bread, and although it was different to the one I was used to, it was almost acceptable and made quite good toast.

'The bakery?' I asked.

She wiped her forehead with her forearm four times, picked something up from the kitchen counter and said, 'No, no. Hand.'

She dropped a key into my upturned palm.

I said, 'You already gave me a—'

'Sea and Land.'

I looked at the small key on the rusty key ring. 'It doesn't look like either of those things.'

My mother laughed. 'The beach hut. Not far from the pier. A little dilapidated, I'm afraid. We can do some renovations at some point. All yours. I have a hunch you'll like it. Drink. Water!'

As I cycled along the beach, I saw a seagull swoop to steal a sandwich from a woman's hand, leaving a streaky deposit on her shirt as it flew away. Which reminded me . . .

My second favourite gull fact is that in World War I, the British army fed herring gulls from periscopes so the gulls would wheel and cry excitedly when they saw an enemy submarine, thinking it brought food. Later they tried training them to excrete on the periscopes so their enemies wouldn't be able to see through the eyepiece. Neither plan worked.

Then I saw her. Ivy. She turned on to the main road towards the pier with a drinks crate on her head and a sign tied around her neck. A huge white shirt was draped over her like a sheet, she had red wellies on her feet and her long dark hair was flapping behind her. I couldn't see her chicken or her dog.

What was she wearing? What was she *doing*?

I followed, stopping a good way off, and then leant on my handlebars to watch. She got off her bike by the arcade, put the crate down, and waved and smiled at the sea as if it were an old friend. Then she looked at the sky, clapped fast and shouted, 'Woohooo. Yessss. You're the best!'

Now, I've been utterly confused in my life. Plenty of times. I can't understand why people keep buying clothes they don't need when the textile industry releases two billion tonnes of carbon emissions a year and 20% of the world's chemicals are used to produce and care for clothing. It mystifies me that anyone can genuinely like watching sports. And I have no idea how someone who was perfectly healthy and loved life could, within three months, be gone for ever.

But this? Waving at the sea? Clapping at the sky?

She propped the bike against the wall and walked down the pier. I didn't follow her. Instead, I set off to find the beach hut, imagining all kinds of friends passing by and popping in to say hello on their long walk along the shore.

19. IVY

The pier is pretty long: 940 planks from beginning to end, which is relevant if you want to imagine how long it is, but unless you know what 940 planks look like in a row, I'm not sure it's all that helpful. At the entrance, there's a mural of George Orwell and a quotation from one of his books. 'All animals are equal, but some are more equal than others.'

That always makes me frown.

Apart from that, I loved the pier. It went out over the waves and stopped way out from the shore. At the end was an open area where on bad days fishermen stood torturing innocent fish, but on good days no one was there except me.

Martin was hushing and slapping far below me: I could see it lurching through the slats. I love the sea, which is why I call it Martin. I think calling it 'the sea' is a bit impersonal. I don't call my dog 'the dog', I don't call Percy 'the friend' and I certainly don't call my teacher 'the teacher'. No. They have names. And something as cosmic, mighty and gobsmacking as the sea should have a name too.

Daddy Jeremy told me the sea in Latin is 'mar', which is the root of the word 'marine'. Mar isn't a great name, but adding 'tin' came to me in this eureka moment. OK, it's not the most wow name in the world (sorry if your name is Martin), and I don't know why it had to be Martin and not Marcia or Marcella, but the sea is obviously not male or female so that doesn't matter. The point is, the sea likes it. It prefers it to being called 'the sea' any day.

I walked to the middle of the pier, placed the crate upside down in front of me like a table or a desk, and propped the sign in front of the crate. I liked it already – it looked all agency-ish and professional.

The sign said:

Ivy Pink Floyd's Animal Action Agency.

Helping creatures big and small with problems big and small.

No fee unless you're rich.

Then I sat down with my legs crossed, the sea wind whipping my hair so it tickled my chin and cheeks, and waited.

I breathed a deep happy lungful of breath. Animals would know they could trust me. The thing coming would know it could trust me. And I was doing something to save the world.

I had never felt so proud.

My agency was born.

20. NATHANIEL

Bees are born twice, I remembered, halfway up the promenade as I crouched down to examine a tired one. First the queen lays an egg in the bottom of a honeycomb cell, and after three days, a tiny larva is born. Then, a few times a day, nurse bees add royal jelly – a white, pudding-like food – to the bottom of the cell, which makes the larva grow big very quickly. Nine days later, the bees put a cap on the larva's cell, which spins into a cocoon and pupates. Twenty-one days after being born the first time, the pupae bee chews the cap off the cell and hatches as a baby bee.

I very much wanted to tell someone this, and looked up to find a lucky person. I was choosing between a very tall man and a lady in a sundress when a not-very-nice-looking boy walked past with a catapult.

'Oi,' he said.

I looked left and right, but he seemed to be addressing me. He was rough and heavy, with spiky blond hair and cruel grey eyes.

'Yeah, you. What you doing?'

Was it a trick question? 'Studying this bee.' I stood up and pushed my glasses up my nose. 'Bees can communicate with each other by dancing.'

'What're you doing *round here*? In that anorak?'

I kept my eyes fixed on the ground, put my hand in my pocket and squeezed my red rubber ball. 'Visiting my mother.' I felt awkward, so I added, 'Honey bees have to fly 90,000 miles, which is three times around the globe, and gather nectar from two million flowers to make one pound of honey, even though the average bee will make only one-twelfth of a teaspoon of honey in its lifetime.'

He laughed. 'This is gonna be fun. And you're hanging around with Weirdo Dolittle? Even better.'

'Who?'

'Thinks she can talk to animals. Saw you talking to her outside the library.'

I felt like defending Ivy and I didn't know why.

'She's off her head,' he said. 'Just like you.' He walked away, kicking his leg towards a dog that had been tied up outside a tea stall, missing it but making it yelp. I stared after him in alarm, then turned quickly, looking for the beach hut. As I read the names with my heart jackhammering, I counted to ten in all eight languages and tried to keep my breathing long and slow.

'Sea and Land' had a stiff padlock on the rust-hinged door, battered by the salty wind and sea spray. I opened the lock and stepped inside.

I never imagined I'd have a beach hut of my own. The white and blue paint was peeling but I didn't mind. The hut had a counter across the back wall topped with a kettle and a stand of mugs, and on the left, a little sink and tap. Yellow-and-white checked curtains were drawn across the windows, so I pulled them back to let the sunlight in. Sketches of lighthouses, starfish and coral hung on the white walls, and propped against one were three folded deckchairs. It was a little cobwebby and dusty, but nothing a dustpan and brush couldn't fix.

I loved it.

I rinsed the dust from a mug, let the tap run and sat on the step facing the beach drinking some water. The heat made me thirsty all the time and no matter how much I drank, I always wanted water. To the left, I could see the sweep of the bay and the pier, and to the right, fishing boats bobbed near the coast and huge grey ships sat further out near the horizon. The sea was deep blue and the sun was blazing.

I wished Grandma had brought me here. Why hadn't she? That seemed mysterious in itself. I reached for my bag, missing her so much my chest hurt. I'd learnt so much from her. Her brain was alert and always busy. She made the world fascinating, alive and full of wonder. I had so much left to learn and discover, but she wasn't here to make it exciting.

Now it was my mother and me, and an odd mystery that was bothering me. My mother had taken something from Mexico that was bad enough to cause Grandma to stop speaking to her, and I couldn't imagine what it might be.

21. IVY

My agency was not the instant success I'd imagined. Dog walkers stared and children laughed at me. Jamie Heggarty came out of the souvenir shop and stood in front of me with her arms crossed.

'Amanda said you can't do that here, and she's the boss,' she said. She looked a bit hostile, so I put the sign in the crate and said, 'I'm protecting animals. You should be on my side.' Jamie goes on protest marches against animal cruelty so you'd think she'd be the last person shooing me away.

'I am. I'm totally with you and whatever you're doing with your little sign and your crate, but I also work here and need the money, so move away right now.'

I marched to the end of the pier, where two fishermen were standing with bags and buckets near their feet, looking vacant. Fishing does that to you. It's like your brain goes on holiday for a while even though it doesn't leave your head. 'Gentlemen, good morning,' I said, marching over. Even if you secretly want to push someone off the pier, you still need to be polite. 'The fish are not happy about—'

'Get lost,' the one nearest me snapped, reeling the wheely thing on his rod. He was bald and the skin on his face and head looked oily, which is not relevant, but it is interesting.

'But they find it disturbing, having hooks stuck in their mouths and being pulled out of the water, even if you put them back in ag—'

'Before I call the manager,' he added.

'The manager of the *sea*?'

He looked at the other man and they laughed.

'But how would *you* like it if—' I began but the other man asked, 'What's with the sign?'

'It's to make my agency look more professional.' He didn't ask 'What agency?' which is what I was hoping for. Instead, he flicked his rod so the line shot out and landed remarkably far away. Maybe if I'd been more forceful about the fish, the men would have stopped trying to catch them and I'd have had my first victory, so that was a bit frustrating.

'THE FISH DON'T LIKE IT!' I shouted, but the men ignored me. 'Put yourselves in their—'

'OI!'

Jamie Heggarty was marching towards me, looking fierce.

'Ivy Pink Floyd, if I catch you here again . . .' she shouted, but she didn't finish her sentence so I'll never know what it was she was going to say. The only way I'll know for sure is if I go back and she catches me again, which I might do tomorrow.

'FISH!' I yelled. 'GET AWAY QUICK! It's a TRAP!'

I couldn't tell whether they heard or not, but they didn't answer, which made me feel bad.

'GO!' Jamie Heggarty snapped.

'Sorry, fish,' I shouted. 'I did try.' I stood for a second, sensing the impossible possible getting nearer and nearer, then turned and trudged down the pier to my bike.

I learnt two important lessons that morning:

1. My agency needed to be in a better location.

2. It's hard to protect creatures because people just don't listen. Unlike goats. They always listen when other goats complain. (It's true. Ask anyone.)

I was running out of time to prove how capable I was. I told the seagulls to stop laughing, put the crate over my head and got on my bike.

22. NATHANIEL

Not far from Huntington House, I saw Ivy swerving towards me on her bike with the crate over her head, yelling, 'Woah-uuu-hhh!'

I tried my best to avoid her but the road was too narrow. She bumped into a kerb, and fell off her bike in front of me so we collided and I fell off mine in a tangle of bikes, crates and signs. The crate bounced on to my foot and her sign bashed me on the temple. 'Arghh!' I yelled. 'How can you possibly see with a—'

'Ayyyiiiieee!' she bawled, clutching her knee. It had a big gritty graze on it and it was bleeding.

'What about my foot? And my head?' I stood up and tried to untangle my bike. A passing family glared at us in alarm and the mother asked, 'Are you two all right?'

'If SOME people looked where they were going, I'd be fine!' Ivy said.

'You're the one cycling with a crate on your head!' I pointed out. 'That's dangerous. Luckily no cars were coming or we could be dead.' The family carried on walking.

I picked up her sign, which said *Ivy Pink Floyd's Animal Action Agency*, and handed it to her.

'That was my idea,' I said, 'and you've gone ahead and set it up without me.'

She frowned and rubbed her knee. 'I work alone.'

'That's not the best way to save the planet,' I pointed out.

'I don't need human help.'

''Course you do. We have to work together to have any chance of making a difference.'

She scowled. 'Aren't anoraks dyed?'

'Yes,' I replied. 'But this one is 100% recycled nylon and all the company's profits go to environmental organizations.'

'Oh.' She rubbed her knee. 'Do you have a creature with a problem?'

'No.'

'Then I don't have time for this.' She picked up her bike, so I quickly said, 'But *I* have a problem.'

'I help *crea-tures*. Not *hu-mans*.'

'I'm a creature.'

'You can solve your own problems,' Ivy said,

brushing her shirt. 'They can't.'

'I really can't. I need your help. I'll pay you.'

Ivy thought about it for a second. 'Hmm. My first paying customer. But you're a *boy* with a problem and not a woodlouse or a rabbit, which was what I was hoping for.'

She was as confusing as my mother. 'Sorry?' I asked.

'I'm not doing this for the money, but fudge isn't free, you know.'

I nodded. 'I have some savings. I can buy you fudge. Will you come to Huntington House tomorrow at ten? It's on Gun Hill.'

23. IVY

I learnt in school that the cannons on Gun Hill aren't on the cliff top so kids can sit on them like horses, tourists can take photos and bored teenagers can smoke by them at night. No. The cannons were put there to protect Southwold from the Dunkirk pirates. That sounds exciting, but if you know Southwold, you'll know it's the least exciting place in the universe for pirate action. What would they steal? Fudge? Ale?

'There's a headless ghost on Gun Hill,' I said. Nathaniel frowned. 'No, really. A soldier called James Martin came to a nasty end in 1842 when the guns were fired for the last time. They were celebrating the birthday of the Prince of Wales at the time. I wish they celebrated *my* birthday by firing cannons but anyway. James Martin was reloading Gun One for a second round and it didn't go off. What should you never, ever do when that happens? Right: you should never go to the front of your cannon and *look down the muzzle*. Even I know that, and I don't own a cannon. But James Martin did exactly that, and it went *boom* and blew his head off, leaving his poor wife with three young children, and Gun Hill with a headless ghost.'

He didn't say anything. He just stood there looking at me.

'No one knows which cannon it is, either, because in World War I, they took them down and buried them so no one would steal them and then put them back on Gun Hill in random order. Gun One could be any of them.'

I didn't want to say no to my first proper agency job, but this was a problem. I said, 'I don't know about you, but I am terrified of ghosts, so I avoid Gun Hill. It makes my hairs stand on end and the blood drain to my boots. I do not want to meet a headless ghost, or even one with a head for that matter.'

'Is that a no, then?' he asked.

I thought about that. 'Is Henny your mother?'

He nodded.

I thought some more. Henny had moved in there not long before, and I liked her because she took in rescue animals.

'Maybe,' I said. 'But you have to tell me more about

ways to save animals by doing random and uncon-
nected things like changing my shirt. And you can
wipe that smile off your face as well. It's like you've
got a toothbrush stuck between your teeth.'

He stopped smiling. 'Is that bad?'

'Obviously.'

I looked up at the sky, so he did too. It needed
more applause, but I wasn't going to do it in front
of him.

'Recycle clothes,' he said quietly, reaching for his
bike. 'Or buy from ethical clothing companies.'

I didn't know what 'ethical' meant, but I wasn't
going to tell *him* that. 'This shirt is recycled,' I said.
'Daddy Jeremy used to wear it for work and now it's
the uniform of an animal action hero.'

'See you tomorrow, then,' he said, pushing his
glasses up his nose, and he cycled off. Which was a bit
abrupt, but whatever.

He must have noticed how unsure the sky was
because he kept looking up at it. No wonder he
crashes into people.

I stashed the crate behind a low wall and picked up
the rest of my stuff. Then I felt it again.

I stopped and listened.

It was coming. Soon.

My knees were stinging and the grazes had grit in

them, but I had more important matters to worry about. In a few days, the impossible possible was going to happen. The impossible possible was going to climb out of Martin (which sounds very strange but that will make perfect sense soon enough) and do something even more impossible.

But that was later.

24. NATHANIEL

'Late, Nathaniel,' my mother said when I entered the kitchen. She saw the cut on my head and added, 'Accident?' The house was stuffy and smelt like socks.

'Ivy crashed into—'

'Lovely girl,' my mother said, opening a cupboard and pulling out a bottle. 'Glad you're friends. Sit.'

'We're not friends,' I said, sitting on a stool. 'She takes her chicken to the libra— arrrrgh.' The antiseptic stung but my mother didn't stop dabbing.

''Course. Every Saturday morning.'

'But why does she read to a chicken?

'Awful childhood.'

'*The chicken?*'

'Ivy. Poor girl. Jellyfish,' my mother said, turning to shush Lola, who was screeching repeatedly.

I was so confused. 'Ivy poor girl jellyfish?'

'No, no. Do keep up. Ivy. Full stop. Poor girl. Full

stop. Different sentence. Jellyfish.' She waved her hand at Lola again. 'Hush, Lola. Swarms of them in the sea. Jellyfish, I'm talking about now. Hot weather's brought them in. Enormous, apparently. Lola! Let's go to the pier later and see them. Bit of an attraction, by all accounts.'

'Which kind?' I asked.

'Of pier?'

'Of jellyfish.'

'Dustbin lids. Or so I hear. Is that a kind?' My mother put the antiseptic away.

'Oh, yes,' I replied. 'Barrel jellyfish. They're the size of dustbin lids, hence the nickname.' Some excellent jellyfish facts came to mind, but I decided not to share them. My animal-fact-telling wasn't going so well. People either weren't interested or they burst into tears. Which reminded me of Ivy. 'What do you mean, "awful childhood"?'

'Long story. I'll tell you later. I have to weed the garden while it's cool.'

While she was out there, I began to look around for whatever it was Grandma said was here for me. There were so many objects in that house that I felt quite tense. After an hour of searching, I found a colourful stripy blanket, an ironwood carving of a bird like the one Grandma bought me from a Seri man years before, and a photo of my mother, aged about seventeen, sitting on the beach with a very young Aunt Nancy. I turned the photograph over. On the back it said, 'Henrietta and Nancy. Mexico.'

I looked at the photograph again, scouring it for clues, but all I could see was a sandy beach and the smiling faces of two quite naughty-looking teenage girls. My eyes turned to the room filled with hundreds of objects. Something was here for me. What was it? It could have been *anything*.

The next morning, I was eating crumpets in my mother's chaotic kitchen with mixed feelings. My mouth was happily producing saliva, which made me think of swifts: during the nesting season, they produce a viscous spit to glue materials together to make a nest. The *Aerodramus* swifts build their nests *only* with saliva and people eat them, Uncle Charles included. He told me that some birds' nest soups can cost thousands of pounds. I was wondering how the first person decided that birds' spit soup would make a good meal when there was a knock at the door.

'Ah. Good,' my mother said as she opened it. 'Toast.'

A familiar voice replied, 'My name's not Toast. It's Ivy.'

My mother chortled. 'I know – I was offering.'

'Yes, please. With jam. Rufus said he'll stay outside. He's not keen on your cats.'

My mother grinned as she led Ivy into the kitchen. 'Hi, Lola,' Ivy said, ignoring me. Lola screeched repeatedly and Ivy replied, 'I know. I saw that, too. Terrible.'

Her pretending to understand Lola made me feel uncomfortable, so I said, 'The collective noun for parrots is a *pandemonium*.'

'Perfect,' she said, smiling at Lola. Lola shrieked raucously, as if to prove the point. 'I wanted to bring you a present,' Ivy continued, talking to Lola as if she were a human, 'but on my way to the harbour to get you a fish head, I met a sad adder and had to make it a happier adder, and by then the fish hut was closed.'

Lola shrieked. I found it all very unsettling, so I said, 'Spiders' muscles pull their legs inwards but to push them out, they pump them with a watery liquid. That's why a dead spider's legs curl up – there's no fluid to extend them again.'

She glowered, said 'Random', and bent down to rub Bessie's ears. Bessie is one of my mother's rescue cats. She's fat and black with orange eyes, and I stay away from her because she hisses at me. She didn't hiss at Ivy. In fact, she seemed to like her, which unsettled me even more.

'Some male spiders give female spiders flies as presents,' I added.

'Nobody better give me a fly as a present,' Ivy said. She turned to my mother and went on, 'Three sets of your neighbours are feeding Bessie.'

'Gosh, no wonder she's fat,' my mother replied.

'She misses hymns,' Ivy said. 'She's very religious, you know. She lived at the vicarage before the vicar moved. Her favourite hymn is "Jerusalem".' She turned to Bessie and sang, *'And did those feeeeet in ancient time walk upon England's mountains greeeenn . . .'*

Bessie jumped on to the table, purring, as Ivy sang on. With a wry smile, my mother laid some toast on the table for Ivy and picked Bessie up. 'No cats on the table. Hymns or no hymns.'

Bessie yowled but Ivy sang louder and louder, sounding, by the end, like a male opera singer. *'. . . Nor shall my sword sleeeep in my hand, till we have builllllt Jeruuuusalem, in England's green and pleasant laaaaand.'* My mother burst into applause and shouted, 'Bravo!' as Ivy sat down opposite me.

I stared at her and then at my mother. What on earth was going on?

Ivy's eyes rested on me in a heavy glare. 'Talking of cats, Gus Burnham tried to drop a kitten down the well last year, but I saw him and stopped him just in time,' she said. 'My last lot of baby frogs weren't so lucky. I'd grown them since they were tadpoles and I was taking them back to the river when he rode past on his bike and hit the jar out of my hands. When it smashed, he leapt off his bike and stamped on them, even though I was screaming at him, until someone came out of a shop and he ran away. Boys,' she said, still death-staring me. 'Mean and horrible.'

'*I'm* not,' I said, avoiding her gaze.

'Nathaniel is lovely,' my mother said. Ivy scowled. She carefully picked the seeds from her toast, one by one, and put them in her pocket. Then she held her toast up to the light, looked through it, put it down and inspected the butter. 'Is this Jim's?' she asked.

'His cows' to be accurate,' my mother answered.

Ivy grinned and spread the butter on her toast in a thick layer. 'I love those cows. Daisy said it's fine if I eat butter made from her milk. I asked her. And Nelly's really good at football, but only because she thinks the ball is her calf so she runs after it and tries to keep it between her legs.'

'Jam,' my mother said. I thought that was an odd response until she pointed to the jar on the table. 'Morello cherry. Excellent.'

Ivy picked up the jam jar. 'Mrs Freeman's?'

'Gwen's,' my mother said.

'Hmm.' Ivy coated one half of her toast in jam, took a bite, then peered into the jar as if she'd lost something in there. 'Not bad. Not as good as Mrs Freeman's, but then she makes the best jam in the universe. So that's your name, is it?'

I assumed she was talking to the jam because she was still inspecting it closely, but then she turned in my direction. 'Nathaniel?'

'Me?' I answered. 'Yes. Nathaniel Breakwell.'

'Actually, his full name,' my mother piped up, 'is The Honourable Nathaniel Charles Alexander Hunt-ington-Breakwell. Not my choice. I wanted to call him "Ocean Sunrise" but my mother wouldn't hear of it.'

Ivy sniggered, which wasn't very nice of her. I kept my head down and squeezed my red rubber ball. It wasn't my fault I had such a long name. 'Bob' would have been fine by me. 'Ocean Sunrise', on the other hand, would not.

'So, Nathaniel Loads-of-Names Breakwell,' Ivy said, leaning back on her chair with a grin I didn't appreciate. 'How can I help?'

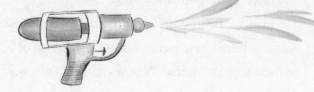

25. IVY

'Ocean Sunrise' didn't suit him one bit, especially as he acted like a robot, which didn't help matters. I couldn't take him seriously. He was stiff, awkward and looked anywhere except right at you, and there's something annoying about that. Then, in the most dramatic voice ever, he said, 'I'm trying to save the planet.'

'Oh. Me too.' I licked the jam off my fingers and he looked completely grossed out.

'You're . . . coating your fingers in your own saliva,' he said.

'Animals,' I said, ignoring him because that was obvious, 'are completely powerless against human beings. They're hunted and splattered and poached, but not in the egg way.'

His mother hooted. I took another bite of toast. 'Their water is being polluted, their food is being

146

sprayed with pesticides, *they* are being sprayed with pesticides –' (by coincidence, I spat crumbs on the table when I said that, but then 'pesticides' *is* quite a spitty word) – 'and they have to deal with oil spills and mobile phone waves and chewing gum, which birds think are pieces of bread and the gum gets stuck in their throats and they die.' I swallowed the toast at that moment, which seemed odd timing. '*They* dream of a better world too, but they can't do much about it. Their habitats are being destroyed all over the place.'

'Yes, but people are taking action. Conservationists in Myanmar are planting a million trees a year by firing seeds at the ground from flying drones,' he replied.

'I did not know that.' I didn't mention that I had no idea where Myanmar was, either.

'I'm going to work in conservation,' he pronounced, which was all very admirable but a very long way off.

'Action needs to be taken now, not when we're twenty-five!' I replied, my eyes wide with impatience and urgency.

'I was thinking more like twenty-one or twenty-two.'

'That's still too late!' I proclaimed, pushing my hair back from my face and getting jam on my cheek.

'Catastrophes are going on out there! Coral is dying and creatures are becoming more and more extinct every day—'

'To be precise, creatures can't get more extinct every day,' he said, his eyes still on the table. 'They're either extinct or they aren't. You mean *species* are becom—'

'—and all because of humans,' I said. 'Look up "How to save the world when you're eleven" on your smartypants phone—'

'It's called a smart phone.'

'Whatever. Bet there's nothing! And there should be.'

'There's plenty we can do to make a difference,' he said. 'Lobby supermarkets to stop selling fruit and veg in packaging. Educate people on the environmental impact of household cleaners. Protect insects. Change light bulbs.'

Henny turned around said, 'Perhaps *we* could, Nathaniel. Do more, I mean. We could . . . greenify this house. Is that a verb? I feel that should be a verb. Where would one start?'

'I have a list upstairs. Grow vegetables, for one,' he said, pushing his glasses up his nose. 'Cut up old sheets to use instead of paper towels, install solar panels, collect rainwater—'

'—use water pistols instead of toilet paper,' she suggested brightly.

I burst out laughing, but I think she was being serious.

'If you want me to help you save the world, that's going to take a lot of fudge. It's not a one-day project. But anyway, I can't. I'm busy.'

'Oh no,' he said. 'I need the services of your agency because I have a mystery to solve.'

'It's an animal action agency – not a mystery-solving agency – so if you don't have an animal with a problem, I can't help you.' His hair was still wet from his bath or shower. (I didn't ask which because it wasn't relevant. See? I totally can tell what's relevant and what isn't.) Just then, I felt it again. The echo and hum of deep open emptiness and an inner push to keep going. 'Can you feel . . .' I paused for ages, my senses alert. A flap and a lap. Endless blues dotted with sprinkles of sunlight. '. . . that?'

He frowned, but he was listening. I could tell because he kept his head very still. Eventually he asked, 'What?'

'That.' I hesitated. Feeling it. 'It's coming. And, believe me, it's . . .' I made hand explosions and detonation sound effects, '*Poccchhh.*'

'What's coming?'

'It'll be here soon and I have to show it I'm totally on its side.'

'Show *what*? What are you talking about?'

I held my finger up for a while, sensing it again. 'That.'

He looked at me blankly. How could he not feel it? But he couldn't so I said, 'You're going to have to hurry up with your mystery.'

He frowned and looked over at his mother. She was cooking something that smelt like baby sick. 'I can't tell you here,' he said. I wasn't sure if she was listening anyway. She's in her own world most of the time, wafting about in long dresses, singing to herself. She's the exact the opposite of him. I can't believe they're even related, even though they have the same blue eyes and they're both extremely posh.

I nodded and said, 'So what's your plan?'

26. NATHANIEL

I didn't have a plan. Obviously saving the world was the predominant plan, but that was a long-term one – I didn't have a specific plan for today.

'Let's go to the hut,' I said. I could talk to her more freely there.

Ivy stood up, pointed at the plate and said, 'Great toast, Henny. Sorry for taking out the seeds but I keep them for the birds. It makes jam squish out of the toast holes, but the birds are so grateful.'

My mother smiled, wriggled her fingers and pointed to the sink. 'Sticky.'

Ivy got the hint and washed her hands as my mother said to her, 'Did you hear that Suffolk has a police tractor, painted like a police car? When the police need a tractor to combat local crime, it tells you rather a lot about the place.'

I left them to chat about sheep theft and went

upstairs to take some money out of my wallet to buy Ivy's fudge. I still had the three pound coins my mother had given me earlier, but I wasn't sure it was enough so I took out two more and went downstairs.

By the time I got to the kitchen, Ivy was singing, 'Don't Worry Be Happy' to my mother's macaw, and Lola was moving from one foot to another. Macaws scream a lot: Lola did it for nearly ten minutes three or four times a day, much to my annoyance. But dancing?

Flies were circling the bare bulb in the kitchen, which reminded me. 'Which light bulbs do you use?' I asked my mother. 'Because replacing one regular light bulb with an LED saves 150 pounds of carbon dioxide a year from entering the atmosphere.'

'The usual, I suppose. I'm happy to change them but you'll have to tell me which ones to buy. Now, Charles and Nancy called to see how you're getting on.' Her tone became a little frosty. She and Aunt Nancy barely spoke on the phone because they always managed to irritate each other. 'They'll ring again this evening.'

I nodded. It was no surprise that they didn't get on. My mother really was infuriating. I didn't trust her, and couldn't cope with her house or her confusing fragments of sentences. I'd encourage her to change her light bulbs, try to discover what Grandma said was here for me, and then ask Charles and Nancy to book me on a train to Sussex, where I'd spend every holiday from now on.

'Let's go,' I said to Ivy.

'OK. Is that you?' she asked, looking at a photograph on the shelf. There were three in a row. The first was of Grandma Ellen in Mexico, standing in a crowded bus station with women wrapped in brightly coloured blankets. The second was of her with Grandpa Aubrey on her wedding day, looking young and happy. The third was of her and me at the seaside. I was about five and holding a spade. We were both smiling.

I nodded and squeezed my red ball. Looking at Grandma, I felt a cavernous pain in my chest. It was hard to believe she was gone.

'It'll take a while, Nathaniel,' my mother said quietly. I kept my eyes on the photograph and squeezed the red ball as tightly as I could until my hand ached. 'Let's go,' I repeated to Ivy, wanting to change the subject before the tears in my eyes rolled down my cheeks.

'OK. If you see Jeremy –' Ivy said to my mother. I didn't know who Jeremy was. I assumed he was a human but it's unwise to assume anything with Ivy –

'please tell him I'm out and about, but I'm very definitely keeping a low profile.'

My mother's head tilted to the side and she said, 'Right.'

As we said goodbye, my mother was smiling for reasons I couldn't comprehend. We set off with Ivy's dog, who'd been waiting outside, across Gun Hill towards the hut.

'Who's Jeremy?' I asked as we walked.

'One of my daddies,' she replied.

'How many do you have?' I didn't have even *one* of those – not properly anyway.

'Only two now. Daddy Jeremy and Daddy Rufus.' She rubbed her dog's ears and added, 'Jeremy's the nicest human in the world, even if his eyebrows do ferret around above his eyes. You get used to it after a while.'

I was confused about the daddies comment, but knew an interesting fact or two about ferrets, so I replied, 'The collective noun is a *business* of ferrets, but seeing as they sleep fourteen hours a day, I can't see how much business is going on.'

She grinned. I was pleased that at least one of my animal facts didn't make her cry. Encouraged, I continued. 'They're crepuscular.'

'Disgusting.'

'Not at all – it just means they're active at dusk or dawn. The noun "ferret" comes from the Latin word *furittus*, which means "little thief", because they hide things away.'

'Well, Daddy Jeremy is not trying to hide his eyebrows away, although that would be interesting. Protection is what they need,' she added.

'His *eyebrows*?'

'*Animals*! Especially the one that's coming. It's relying on me. I've never met one before and I can't mess up. You know, before Joey, I didn't know what to do with my skill. What exactly *can* you do when a cat tells you she's lonely? Tell the owner, sure, and they look at you like you're crazy. But Joey changed my life.'

'Who's Joey?' I asked. 'Another daddy?'

'No, but this is relevant,' she said with a deep sigh. '100%.'

As we walked down to the hut she told me about her experience with a talking hamster. Now deceased.

27. IVY

'Do you talk to *all* animals or just hamsters?' he asked, blinking at me as if he'd just met a singing cricket ball.

I rolled my eyes. Here we go. '*They* talk to *me* as well, you know. It's not just one-way.'

Ducks quacked duck facts at me as we passed, and now and then, an eel wheeled to the surface of the stream, making the water flicker, ripple and splish. The sky was deep blue and happier today. It wasn't the usual kind of weather, where it looked like it would rain as soon as you opened your picnic.

I told Nathaniel about Joey, which made me furious all over again until I was stomping along the road, growling, 'Seriously, humans are the worst creatures alive. This planet was once our home *and* their home, and now it's all about us and they're suffering and dying and have no hope of winning their part of the world back. THE WORLD IS FULL OF TERRIBLE PEOPLE!'

A woman walking past pulled her grandson away from me when I said that. 'Not you,' I said to her, and then glared at her son. 'But maybe.'

'There are plenty of good ones,' Nathaniel said. 'Who care.'

'Pfff.' I carried on stomping. 'No one cares! Not really.'

We stopped at the sweet shop. He didn't move.

'Umm . . . we need to actually go in if we want to buy something. That's how most shops work,' I explained.

'I don't like shops. I don't go in unless I have to.'

'Ohhh-kayyy,' I said, stretching my eyes wide. I left him there by the window, went in, chose my fudge and stuck my head out of the door. 'Do you want anything?'

He pointed to one of the plastic jars in the window. 'What are they?'

'Er . . . cola bottles,' I said making a face because, seriously, what planet was he from?

'And those?'

'Pear drops. Iced caramels. Rhubarb and custards.' I pointed to a few. There were shelves of them – I wasn't going to name them all.

His eyes scanned the shelves. I thought he was choosing until he said, 'Couldn't all these containers be made of something other than plastic?'

'*What?*'

'It's *nefarious.*'

That's what happens when you go to a posh school. You use words like 'nefarious' when you're not even a teenager yet. I had no idea what it meant but when you live with Daddy Jeremy, you get used to working things out, and 'nefarious' definitely didn't mean something cheery.

I gazed at the jars and imagined them all bobbing in the sea for evermore, washed up on shores, creating sweetie-jar mountains in places where no sweetie-jar mountain should ever be. 'Do you want something or not?' I asked, feeling despondent.

He shook his head and handed me some pound coins. It was all a bit back-and-forth, to be honest. He could have just come in and saved me all the faffing about. I paid for the fudge and gave Nathaniel back the change, which he zipped into a pocket in his anorak. Which he still had on, even though it was boiling.

I'd finished most of the fudge by the time I got to the hut. I tried to eat it slowly but if you know what kind of fudge I mean, you'll know it's impossible.

Nathaniel didn't want any. He eyed the plastic wrapper, and in a flash, I pictured the plastic wrappers on all the sweets in that one shop, and then in every shop all over the country and the world, and then all the packaging covering all the other food products in the supermarket and every bottle and even the lids on the cardboard drink cartons and I added all of those to the bobbing sweetie jars in the sea, and suddenly lost my appetite.

He opened the padlock and we went in. It was cool in there, and I mean that in both ways. I was so thirsty, my tongue felt like the old towel Aisling uses to wipe Rufus's muddy paws.

'Is that water drinkable?' My voice was gluey because of the fudge.

He nodded, found a camping cup and turned on the tap.

'What do we do about all the plastic? Not eat fudge? Not eat AT ALL? How can I save animals if I'm starving?'

'You don't need to starve. We just need to do practical things that make a difference,' he said, filling the cup.

'But nobody does.' I glugged the water down, gave some to Rufus and handed Nathaniel the cup back. He stared at it, a little horrified. I'm not sure he's used to sharing a cup with a dog father.

'They say they'll do stuff but they don't,' I went on. 'They say they care but they don't *really*. If they did, they'd make sure the seas were clean and stop making so much noise that insects and birds don't like and *do something*.'

'I don't know who you mean by "they",' Nathaniel replied. 'I only know about me. And I care. Most people do.'

'Huh. Humans. I don't need humans,' I said.

'You do, actually. By working together, we'll save a lot more animals than you could on your own.'

Unlikely, I thought, but I didn't say that.

Nathaniel opened the double doors wide like the pages of a giant book, and spent ten minutes trying to reposition the deckchair while I helped with instructions that were mainly wrong. Beyond the hut door, people walked arm in arm along the beach, their dogs chasing seagulls and sniffing each other's butts excitedly. Butt sniffing is so much fun. I haven't tried it myself but dogs have told me. Families in shorts walked with crab nets in buckets, which reminded me to go down to the harbour later to check the crabs were OK. They love the bacon but they get fed up of being stuck in a bucket for ages with a bunch of crabs that support rival football teams. It can get nasty, even though I tell them all the time that there's more to life than football.

'You have an hour of my time,' I said, once he'd put the deckchair up. To have any chance of staying with Jeremy and Aisling for ever, I had to be there for the creature, but quietly, without anyone knowing. And that was going to be tricky.

I gulped. I wished I hadn't eaten the fudge so quickly.

'I have stuff to do,' I said. 'So you'd better start.'

He nodded, pulled a letter from his anorak and began with his story.

28. NATHANIEL

Ivy pulled at a thread in her shorts and listened. She was sprawled rather inelegantly on the deckchair. I wasn't sure we'd put it up properly and expected it to collapse at any moment, but she didn't seem worried. Rufus slept beside her in the shade of a beach umbrella I'd found inside.

'What did she take?' Ivy asked. 'From Mexico?' She meant my mother.

I shrugged. 'Grandma didn't tell me. She just said she took something, that there was something here for me, and asked me to spend time with my mother.'

'Did your Grandma write Henny a letter?'

I nodded.

'What did it say?'

'*I* don't know. She wrote it for my mother!'

Ivy swung her legs. 'I'd totally read it, but I'm nosy. You know, I see people sitting in these huts every summer. I never thought *I'd* ever sit in one. I feel like a Very Important Pelican. That dog is too hot.' She pointed to a shaggy mongrel on a lead, panting.

'I could have told you that,' I said. It had to be over thirty degrees that day.

'Yeah, but you couldn't have told me her front left foot aches and she's madly in love with a whippet.'

I stayed quiet. I couldn't prove that either way. Further down the beach, a woman let her dog drink from her water bottle. I very much hoped she wasn't going to drink from it herself afterwards. Dog owners seemed to have the strangest hygiene habits.

'So your mother and aunt took something from Mexico, which made your Grandma angry, and they stopped talking to each other—'

'Not only because of that. There were other reasons, but that was the last straw.'

'—and now you want to find the thing she took?'

'Yes. Or at least know what it was.'

'Right.'

'And know what Grandma meant when she said something's here for me.'

Ivy frowned. 'Maybe it's the same thing?' She waved hello to a pigeon, like she'd just seen her classmate on the beach, and then sighed. 'I don't really know how to help you. I'm used to ladybirds with boyfriend issues, and foxes feeling unloved. Did you ask your aunt?' Ivy asked.

'Yes, but she changed the subject. She and my mother don't get along.'

'Why not?' Ivy wafted her huge shirt like a sail and I squeezed the blue ball in my pocket.

'They're very different. They irritate each other. But my mother is eccentric, messy and confusing – she'd irritate anyone.'

We were silent for a moment and then Ivy pulled her ear. She had a strange expression on her face. 'I think she's lovely,' she said.

'You clap at the sky and communicate with hamsters,' I reminded her. 'You're not the best judge of character.'

''Least you have one,' she said. 'When I'm bigger and I go and find mine, I hope she'll be just like Henny. But a Thai version, obviously.'

I felt odd then. I didn't say anything for a long while and neither did Ivy. Perhaps I'd misjudged my mother. After all, Grandma did encourage me to come and spend time with her. But what had happened between the three of them? Something certainly had, and no one was being honest with me.

On the beach directly in front of us, children dug tunnels from the sea to the beach. I had suggestions for the best course of water flow, but I kept them to myself. After a while, Ivy turned to me, her hand shielding her eyes from the sun, and asked, 'Ice cream?'

'What about it?'

'Mine's a Whippy with a Flake.'

'Are you asking me to buy you one?'

'I don't have any money. That's another rubbish thing about being eleven: you have to rely on adults for cash. I don't know about you but I can't wait to earn my own and spend it how I like.'

'Meanwhile you'll spend *mine* how you like?'

'It's like ... part of my wages.' She winked.

I handed her the coins I had left.

'Don't you want one?' she asked.

I shook my head. Ice cream involves tongues and saliva. The very thought of it makes me feel ill. She skipped to the small cafe near the hut, bought a Whippy with a Flake, then sat down beside me to watch the holidaymakers on the beach. I deliberately turned my head. The whole idea of her licking it in circles, her saliva surrounding the entire surface, made me feel very nervous but I didn't say anything because it was pleasing indeed to be sitting outside my new beach hut with a friend.

29. IVY

The ice cream tasted like the inside of a nervous cloud: cold, creamy and anxious about being vanilla flavour. I couldn't understand why Nathaniel didn't want one, but I never did understand boys. I was wondering why he'd hired my services and I was trying to be professional (not everyone can resist the power of fudge). But I really needed life to go back to its normal state where I was friends with creatures, did everything I could to make their lives better, and avoided boys at all costs.

'Right,' I said, popping the last bit of the cone into my mouth and licking the ice-cream dribbles off my fingers. Nathaniel didn't look all that well. I wiped my hands on my shirt and he looked even more queasy.

'Cones are excellent ice-cream holders, aren't they?' I said, having a sudden realization. 'No plastic at all. If carrier bags were made of wafers, we could eat them after we unpacked the shopping.'

'They'd break,' he said.

'Hmm. Let's go and talk to Jeremy and Aisling. They've lived here for years. They know everyone and everything that's ever happened in this town, so I'm pretty sure they'll know about your family.'

'Are they hamsters, too?' he asked.

I laughed. Mainly because if they were creatures, they'd definitely be polar bears. 'They're my foster parents.'

'Why have you got foster pa—'

'Not relevant.' I carried the deckchair into the hut and put it down in a flat, crumpled tangle of wood and cloth. Nathaniel blinked at it a few times, then padlocked the hut door.

I made him stand by the front gate while Rufus and I went in.

You should know about our house. Of course it's relevant. How could you think otherwise? It's one of those old wooden houses on Ferry Road, opposite the dunes, leading from the high street to the harbour. Wide fields sit behind it towards the water tower, and beyond you can see the estuary and the church steeple in Walberswick in the far distance.

The house has three bedrooms: one for Jeremy and

167

Aisling, one for me, and one for devices that belong in museums, like cream-making pumps, sugar nippers and porridge spurtles. They call it 'the guest room', but those things *are* the guests, really. When I moved in, Daddy Jeremy took the locks off the doors (except the front and back, obviously) so I wouldn't feel sad, which is kind of him. He's like that.

My bedroom has a wide window looking on to the garden and a spider living in the corner called Archimedes the Arachnid. (I just call him Archie. I wanted to call him Fang McPoisonbite but he didn't like it. He already has problems making friends – he's super shy and people don't usually like him, and as he rightly pointed out, a name like that doesn't help.)

Anyhow. The wooden floors were painted white about a century ago, but are now only white in the corners. A threadbare Persian rug (my flying carpet when I was young) sits in the middle, and my double bed has four ornate posts topped with brass knobs, so it creaks like a coffin door when I get in. That's spooky because Aisling inherited the bed when her mother died (she didn't die *in* the bed – I asked). Aisling also inherited a wooden wardrobe with access to Narnia through the back and a matching chest of drawers so stiff and heavy that if I don't have energy in the morning, I go the entire day without socks.

Daddy Jeremy was in his armchair reading with the radio on low. He looked up when he saw me and smiled. I felt a latch in my stomach catch. I loved him so much I didn't really know what to do with it all.

'There's a . . . boy outside,' I said. 'He needs help. Can I bring him in?'

'A *boy*?'

'Yes.'

'Really?'

'Yes.'

'Who is he?'

'Holidaymaker. I'm helping him, which means I'm making human friends my own age and not annoying people, just like you asked.'

Daddy Jeremy's eyebrows had the most exercise they'd had in weeks, and that's saying something. He placed his open book face down on the coffee table and stood up, his knees clacking like maracas. 'Won't create a rumpus, will it?'

'Unlikely.'

'Jolly good.'

I didn't like to tell Daddy Jeremy that the most gargantuan rumpus was just around the corner. Instead, I gulped and asked, 'What if it was a *good* rumpus? One that saved lives and helped the planet? That wouldn't be so awful, would it?'

'I think you'll find that even the tiniest rumpus would unacceptably disturb the harmony of our world—'

'—which is why we won't be causing any rumpus *at all*,' I added, my stomach sinking like a rock falling from a tree on to the windscreen of a car, making it splinter into an intricate mosaic, which unfortunately I know about.(Look, I'd climbed up to watch this uh-may-zing caterpillar and I was holding the rock I'd found on the beach that was perfect for the fish in Jake's pond to hide under, and it slipped out of my hand. And yes, I could have left the rock at the foot of the tree (and believe me, I wished I had) but for whatever reason I didn't. The neighbours at 57 weren't very happy about it, because they'd only just bought that car from www.timeforanewcar.com (the sticker was in the back window) and they got a bit irate.)

I led Daddy Jeremy to Nathaniel via the back garden. (Why use the front door when you can see flowers and fields if you go the back way?) Dot ran to me, squawking, but I told her it wasn't library day today. Hens have no sense of time. They really should start making hen calendars.

'Jeremy Goddard,' Daddy Jeremy said kindly, shaking Nathaniel's hand. He looked and sounded like David Attenborough. I wished he was, sometimes, but

170

Daddy Jeremy was a life-saving legend in his own way. 'How do you do?'

'Pleased to meet you,' Nathaniel said, sounding like a businessman. 'I believe you knew my grandmother, Professor Ellen Huntington? And my grandfather, Aubrey?'

'Indeed,' Daddy Jeremy replied. 'Lord and Lady Huntington. Very agreeable people.'

LORD? I thought. *LADY?*

'You're Henrietta's boy, aren't you?' Jeremy asked. 'How might I be of assistance?'

'Some time ago, my grandmother, mother and aunt fell out. I don't know why. They stopped talking to each other, so it must have been bad,' Nathaniel said. 'Perhaps you know something about it?'

Jeremy's eyebrows squirrelled and ferreted, weaselled and badgered, ottered and voled. Four of those are verbs in English and the last two aren't. Don't ask me why.

'Your Aunt Nancy caused a bit of a scene on the beach, I recall,' Jeremy said. 'Twenty-five years or so ago, now.'

Daddy Jeremy's eyes are as pale and grey as a January puddle. They rested on me for a while, and I was grateful I was wearing my wellies. 'Delighted to meet you,' he said to Nathaniel, and he turned towards the house.

'Daddy Jeremy,' I said, knowing Nathaniel would not be satisfied with an answer like that, 'could you possibly elucidate?' I felt like one of them: posh, clever and extremely polite. I'm not any of those things, but I can confirm that speaking like that makes your mouth feel happy.

'Wonderful woman, your grandmother,' Jeremy said, facing Nathaniel. 'Your Aunt Nancy, too. Keen on safeguarding animals – rather like you, Ivy.' He peered at me. Peering is different from looking, as far as I can tell: it's more like an exam you need to pass but the examiner is asking all the questions with his eyes. ''Course, it caused a rather large rumpus, and we are loath to initiate another of those, are we not?'

That's how he speaks, I promise you. He sounds like a textbook written by Prince Charles with the help of Enid Blyton. He also says things like, 'I rather think I'd prefer broccoli this evening,' and, 'would you mind awfully if I were to retire?' when he wants to go to bed. He might sound like he's a hundred and forty years old, but he's only fifty-six. That's one of the reasons they nearly didn't let him and Aisling foster me – they're quite old. Eileen, my social worker, thought I needed to be with a younger family with children, and she was still keen to move me. Attracting the wrong kind of attention might speed up the process.

Daddy Jeremy turned to Nathaniel and smiled. 'Young man, it's been a pleasure.' And he walked along the garden path towards the house, leaving an even bigger mystery behind him than there was before.

30. NATHANIEL

Ivy's foster father was acting very suspiciously, which was a mystery in itself. 'What does he mean about Aunt Nancy "safeguarding animals"?' I asked.

'Even I don't know what he's talking about,' Ivy said, looking at his back as he entered the house, 'and I'm usually good at this. He wasn't very helpful, was he?'

'No.'

'We're getting nowhere,' Ivy said.

I was afraid she'd say, 'Well, that's the end of that, then,' and ask me to leave, which I didn't want to happen. Not when I was enjoying being with Ivy so much, and having a friend was a new experience for me. So I said, 'Your garden has lots of possibilities for taking action.'

'What kind of possibilities?' she asked, gazing around the garden.

'You could make a quiet spot in that corner. A sort of . . . retreat for creatures. You could build a small motel for tired insects. A bus shelter for migrating birds. A worm spa. Things like that.'

She laughed loudly, her long black hair shining like patent leather in the sunshine. 'Brilliant. Totally doing that. Right. This is all a bit of a waste of time, isn't it? So I'm going to walk to the beach, find creatures to help along the way, and prepare for the big thing that's coming.' And she walked quickly out of the front gate, her too-large red wellies flupp-lupping on the pavement.

'*Waste of time?* I thought we were—'

'Nope. We're done. If you want, we can stop at Mr Bumstead's on the way.'

'Mr *Who*?'

'He died!' she cried, not seeming in the least sad about his demise or mine. 'But his shop is still there!'

31. IVY

As shops go, Mr Bumstead's is quite interesting. It's on the corner near the lighthouse and it sells a variety of random things, like butter buns and wool for knitting and baked beans with sausages inside and broken bits of chocolate in a tub. Even though Mr Bumstead is no longer there, Mrs Bumstead hasn't changed the name of the shop to 'Mrs Bumstead's'. I have no idea why.

She has dyed orange hair, and that day she was wearing matching lipstick, which rimmed her glass of iced water in a lip-shaped glob. Nathaniel stared at it. I think he has a problem with mouths and lips.

On the way over, he'd tried to talk me out of cancelling our job contract, but Rufus and I weren't interested. We had bigger tofu to fry.

'Mrs Bumstead,' I said, 'did you know—?'

'Do you know what manners are, young lady?' Mrs

Bumstead snapped, folding her arms over her huge, sticky-out chest that looks like a shelf to rest your glasses and your book on.

I corrected myself. '*Hello*, Mrs Bumstead.'

'Hello, Ivy.'

'Did you know someone called Lady Ellen Huntington?'

''Course. Professor, wa'n't she?'

I nodded. 'She was his grandmother.'

'Oh, you're Lady Henrietta's son, are you?' Mrs Bumstead asked, turning to Nathaniel. 'Heard you were here. Yes, 'course I knew your grandmother. Nice lady. Clever as anything. Wore colourful shawls and bought lots of tinned pineapples. Naughty daughters, though. Argued with their mother and got up to all kinds of hijinks. One of them caused a right commotion at the beach, years ago. Quite upset Mr B, she did.'

'Commotion?' Nathaniel asked.

'Up to something. Digging and whatnot. Mr Bumstead didn't like it.'

'Digging?' I looked at Nathaniel with a frown. 'What kind of commotion?'

'Camped on the beach near the dunes, she did. Stayed a few weeks, and wouldn't let any dogs come near. She shouted at Frank Zappa – Mr Bumstead's

Highland terrier. Yanked him by the collar to get him away and everything. Took offence, Mr Bumstead did. I forget the details now but she got the whole town talking. Not much goes on in this town, and they were nobility, so word got round quick enough. Everyone thought she was cuckoo. My Meg was in her pushchair, and she's twenty-seven next month.'

Nathaniel's eyes still hadn't left her glass of water. It was starting to be weird. She looked at him and I looked at him, and then I nudged him, and instead of looking away, like a normal person, he said, 'Nearly 3% of Antarctic glaciers is penguin urine.'

My eyes widened and Mrs Bumstead turned pale.

Then I remembered he didn't like going into shops. Maybe that was the problem. 'What was Henny doing?' I asked, trying to change the subject rapido. 'On the beach?'

Mrs Bumstead looked at me and said, 'Oh, it weren't Henrietta on the beach. It was the older one.'

'*Nancy?*' Nathaniel asked.

'That's the one. No one knows what she was doing – that's why it caused all the talk. My guess is, she quarrelled with her beau. Stiff-looking bloke, he was.'

'But . . . why camp on the beach?' I persisted. 'And why shoo dogs away?'

'Probably allergic. Does Jeremy know you're

snooping around?'

I laughed. '*Snooping!* I was just introducing my new friend here to Mrs Bumstead.'

Nathaniel's eyes finally left the glass and almost landed on me. Almost. 'Did you say "friend"?' he asked. Then he looked really happy with himself. He was so weird.

'That tangerine lipstick is gorgeous!' I said to Mrs Bumstead, trying to cover up for him yet again. 'You look *lovely*.'

'Oh, thank you – it's called "Heatwave", funnily enough.' Mrs Bumstead checked her lips in the mirror behind the counter.

'You won't tell Jeremy I was in here asking questions, will you?' I asked in my sweetest voice.

'Go on, the pair of you. 'Course not.'

'Thank you, Mrs Bumstead!' I cried, and pulled Nathaniel's anorak by the elbow towards the door.

'Her lipstick was hideous,' he said once we were out and had crossed the road. 'Why did you—?'

'You don't know how to get the best out of people, do you?'

He thought about it. 'No.'

I rolled my eyes. Seriously, this kid. I rubbed Rufus's ears and said, 'Listen, you can't keep doing that. You have to stop telling people random facts about penguin wee.'

He stood still. Rufus stopped too, so I had to as well. Nathaniel blinked a few times with that serious face he has 100% of the time, and said, 'I only told *her* that.'

'You know what I mean. Stop with all the random fact-telling! It's weird. That's why you don't have any friends. You scare people away.'

He frowned and said bluntly, 'You're the one who talks to animals.'

'Yes! And animals talk to me – it's not just one-sided, you know. But I'm not the one who wants human friends – you are.'

'Aunt Nancy isn't allergic to dogs,' he said, his eyes fixed anywhere but on me. 'She has two at home. What could she have been doing at the beach?'

'I wonder if . . .' I began, tilting my head to one side. I stopped walking and stood thinking, squeezing my eyes together to help my brain focus, but it could-n't because suddenly I had this overwhelming wave wash over me and all my body started tingling. The echo and hum of deep open emptiness. The inner push to keep going. The flap and lap. The endless blues dotted with sprinkles of sunlight. 'Can you *really* not feel it?' I asked. 'It's so close! It'll be here any day!'

'Feel *what?*'

'I wonder if they're related,' I added.

'*You wonder if who's related?* Ivy, I already have a mother who makes no sense – I don't need a friend who makes no sense as well.'

'Urrrgggh!' I yelled. 'The thing that's coming and your aunt.' And I started running down the steps to the beach.

Summer was snuggling the town like a giant yellow beanbag of light and heat and squish. Seagulls were making announcements and telling each other dad jokes, and flying ants kept landing on my hair.

I shook my head hard. Mainly to get two flying ants out, but also because I couldn't believe what was on its way. This was CURRAZZY. Excited, I yelled, *I'm here! I'll help you! COME!* (but this time I said it aloud).

Nathaniel stood watching me, shaking his head. I know because I turned around and yelled at him not to follow me.

Down on the beach, bucket-and-spadey stuff was going on. Sunlight dazzled on the sea like blinding glitter, making me wish I had sunglasses to protect my eyes from sparklyitis. Parents played boules on the sand and pretended to be rubbish to let their children win. Toddlers held fistfuls of sand with evil looks on their faces. Giggling kids with spades buried their dads while their mothers read books on folding chairs with dogs tied to the legs. It would have been quite lovely if the planet's creatures were all doing OK. Except they weren't.

'Wait!' Nathaniel said, running after me.

'Enough! I have work to do!'

But he ran ahead and stood in front of me, making me stop. 'Please,' he said. 'Don't keep running off.'

'You need to talk to your Aunt Nancy. Ask her about the commotion at the beach. I don't have time for this. I could have helped lots of animals today and instead, I've been on a wild goose chase with you. Which isn't a nice phrase because it doesn't sound fun for the poor wild goose. I quit.' I turned my head left and right, wondering who and what was nearby and might need some help.

'But . . . I hired you . . . your agency . . . the fudge,' he stammered.

'Money's the reason the world is in this mess. I can't be one of those people who puts fudge or money before the needs of others. Animals need me – and anyway, a gigantic one is just about to arrive.'

'A gigantic what? What are you *talking* about?'

I stood statue-still, feeling it, my eyeballs darting with alertness. 'That.'

He stared at me. Ten seconds went by. Three trees were chopped down in the Amazon rainforest. A two-headed snake hatched from an egg in the Congo. A dog in a park in Putney sniffed a new sniff and went wild with elation. And the creature got closer.

Nathaniel's wintry face didn't match the cheerful summer beach scenes, but he was not high on the list of sad creatures I needed to help. He was near the bottom, in fact. But when he said, 'Ivy, please,' he looked so sad, I gave in.

'Fine. I'm pretty sure it's a turtle,' I said. 'I've never spoken to one before, so I don't know if I'm right, but when I add up all the clues it *has* to be.'

'A *turtle*?'

'A huge one. Coming. Here. Soon.' I paused between the words, but he still looked at me blankly.

'Turtles live in tropical seas,' Nathaniel pointed out.

'Yep, clever old them. Soon as I can, I'm moving to the tropics myself.'

He looked puzzled. 'But why would a turtle be com—'

'I'll take the fudge and the ice cream as payment for today,' I said. 'Come on, Rufus.'

'You said I was your friend,' Nathaniel said, quietly. 'Friends help each other.'

Rufus stopped and looked at me accusingly.

'Ohhh.' I smiled kindly (to Rufus, but to Nathaniel, too). 'I was just—'

I didn't want to tell him, but I could never be friends with a boy. If I *ever* could, it would probably be with someone like him, but then again, maybe not. Squirrels and eels were a lot more fun. 'Good luck, though.'

I set my animal antennae twingling to let creatures know I was back in business, and I strolled away into the happy sunshine.

32. NATHANIEL

'Oh dear – not very happy? Tea?' my mother offered when I walked in looking glum. She wiped her hands on one of the old towels over the banister. Her face was red, as if she'd been hauling things around. She was wearing a green embroidered shirt and shorts, and her hair was coiled back in a clip with damp strands clinging to her neck. 'Iced, I should think. Sweltering today. Come.' The piles of laundry and dishes had gone, but boxes lined the walls and old hardback books stood in towers in the hallway.

'I'm not a tea drinker,' I said, counting to ten and squeezing the red ball to quell the panic of the mess.

'Something else? Water? Gin?'

My eyes stretched. 'Water, please.'

She ambled to the tap, stretching her arms to the sides and above her head, and filled a glass. I wasn't sure if I'd heard correctly so I sat at the table, feeling downcast.

'I wasn't serious about the gin,' my mother said, handing me the glass. 'Just a little joke. I don't drink alcohol at all. One doesn't, in the ashram, and now I've no interest in it or its energy. Please don't relay that comment to my sister – she does not share my sense of humour. Runner beans.' She pointed to a basket of them. 'Jim gave us four kilos. Perhaps we could be vegan.'

Lola attacked a wooden toy with her beak, distracting us both. 'I don't agree with keeping birds in captivity,' my mother murmured. 'Creatures should be free and live in their natural habitats, but for birds, it's even worse. I'd never have done this to poor Lola. Ferdinand.'

'Sorry?'

'At the animal sanctuary. He called saying he needed a home for her. Since I got back from Dharamsala, they always call me first.'

I didn't know where Dharamsala was but it sounded exotic.

'Her owner abused her. Starved her, neglected her. Awful. I couldn't let that continue.' She gave Lola a sunflower seed and I wondered how anyone could do that to a beautiful bird like Lola. She had a gangster attitude and was riotously noisy at times, but she was very affectionate to my mother, and lots of fun when she wasn't screaming or sneezing. I was still terrified of her because she kept lunging at me and then pulling away, but my mother said she was playing with me to see my reaction. I didn't want to risk it, so I kept my distance.

'One day at the ashram,' my mother went on, 'I realized it was time to take responsibility.' Her eyes drifted gracefully towards me, then drifted back to Lola. 'Love and compassion aren't measured on a scale of importance. Small acts are as worthy as great ones. Aren't they, Lola?'

Lola sneezed loudly. She did it regularly to clear her nostrils, but this time it seemed like confirmation.

'Are you all right?' my mother asked. 'You look—'

'I need to lie down.'

I put the empty glass on the table, climbed the stairs and lay spread-eagled on my bed in the heat. Ten minutes later, my mother knocked at the door. When I grunted, she came in holding a plate with a sandwich.

'Cheese,' she said, setting the plate on the bedside table and lifting her arms to cool herself down. She seemed like a bird herself when she did that. 'From Jim, wrapped in a cloth, not in plastic. I found the bread you like. No spaces between the cheese slices.

What's the matter?'

'Ivy doesn't want to be my friend.' I curled in a ball on the bed.

My mother sighed and sat down on the chair near the dresser. 'Trauma runs deep, Nathaniel. She has issues with trust.'

'I don't know what that means.'

'Well, her father terrorized them both – Ivy *and* her mother, who's Thai, by the way, hence Ivy's—' my mother circled her face with her finger, indicating Ivy's general look. 'When she was five, her father met someone else and had her mother convicted and deported for a theft I doubt very much she committed. He was sent to prison soon afterwards for being equally awful to the new partner. Ivy ended up in a children's home.'

I was quiet for a while and then asked, 'Is that why she's fostered?'

'Yes. And, one of the first things Jeremy and Aisling did was take her to a rescue home for animals, where she chose—'

'Rufus.'

'Exactly.'

'And Dot?'

'No, Dot's a more recent friend of hers. I believe Ivy hatched Dot herself by wrapping the egg in her woolly hat.'

My mother went quiet and I lay thinking about that. The fan whirred, sending loops of hot air around the room. Beyond the window, birds tweeted, warbled, clucked and made rattlesnake noises, and someone walking by coughed loudly. Inside, flies buzzed around the frilly light fitting. My mother was quiet for so long, I thought she'd gone out. I opened an eye to check, but she was still sitting there, her eyes on the cows.

'Nathaniel,' she said softly, 'in some circumstances, people other than parents raise a child. You lived with Grandma, and Ivy lives with the Goddards. Jeremy and Aisling were strangers to Ivy once, just as I am to you, but they're a perfect fit and they're happy together. And I very much hope we will be, too.'

'OK.' I wasn't so sure about that myself, but 'OK' seemed the best answer in uncomfortable circumstances. 'Why are people cruel to one another?' I asked after a moment.

'I don't know,' my mother said gently, shifting her weight on the chair and making it squeak. 'Cruelty is beyond my understanding. But what I do know is that sometimes good people do bad things.'

'Did you?' I asked. 'Do bad things?'

She smiled. 'Of course. We all—'

'What kind of bad things?'

'Oh, a range. From trivial to rather significant.'

'Like take something you shouldn't have?'

Her chin lowered and she sighed loudly. 'Yes.' After a pause, she added, 'And leave something I shouldn't have.'

'Like?'

She smiled sadly, and said, 'You.'

I felt awkward suddenly, so I sat up and said, 'Cows make 40,000 jaw movements a day, and create 125 pounds of spit. That's like 125 bags of sugar. Most of their energy goes on chewing and producing enough saliva to carry on eating.'

She looked at the cows, her eyes filling with water.

'Holstein–Friesians are called Holsteins in America but Friesians here,' I went on. 'They produce more milk than any other breed: nearly 3,000 gallons a year when they're lactating. An American Holstein called "Selz-Paelle Aftershock 3918" set a new world record in 2017 when she produced 9,380 gallons – more than three times the usual amount.'

My mother dabbed her eyes and angled her head. 'Bizarre name. Do all cows have names like that?'

I shrugged.

'Why did Thingy Aftershock produce so much milk? Do other animals have bumper years? Do bees

190

suddenly have furious bouts of honey production or hens of egg laying?'

I didn't know. But the mention of eggs reminded me of Ivy, and the fact that I was on my own now. 'What did you take from Mexico?'

My mother stood up. 'It was a long time ago. And it's over. I want to put it behind me. I've argued with Grandma and Nancy about it for years and . . . other things . . . and I'm—' She stopped, breathed rather aggressively, and then cleared her throat.

After a short silence, I asked, 'Why don't you finish your sentences? You cut out all the most important information.'

'The important information is,' she paused to push her hair back with her orange plastic sunglasses, 'that all those years we quarrelled and grew apart, we could have spent together. And that's . . . well, it's heartbreaking.'

I didn't know what to say. I was going to mention newts because it sprang to mind, but then she murmured, 'Shame, really. If only it *were* to happen. It would be wonderful.'

She made no sense. My mattress was unbearably hot and my T-shirt was sticking to my back, so I pulled it away and swung my legs so they hung off the edge of the bed. A yellowy mist of waning sunlight lit the dry fields and bushes down to the marshes. I realized, looking at the sandwich, that I was extremely hungry.

A Holstein-Friesian mooed again in the field outside, and I hoped it wasn't because she could smell the cheese.

'You're doing it again,' I muttered. 'If only *what* were to happen?'

She did a nose-laugh that sounded like a short snort. 'Nothing. Sandwich, Nathaniel. She really needs a friend.'

'The *sandwich*?'

'Ivy. You do too.' She walked towards the door. 'Perhaps . . . I don't know. Perhaps it's just not the right time.'

33. IVY

To make up for lost time, I ran home saying, 'I love you,' to every creature I met on the way. When I got there, I hugged Dot, lay on my bed and told Archimedes the Arachnid how Nathaniel had distracted me from my mission but now I was back on track.

'Is he too big for my web?' Archie asked. 'I could wrap him up for you.'

'Kind of you to offer,' I relied, 'but he is. How about you, Archie? Made any friends today?' Poor Archie. Most creatures avoid him. It's not easy being a spider.

'Oh, yes,' Archie said. 'A mosquito and a housefly. Both pleaded with me to free them, but I just couldn't, you see. Although it becomes a little lonely when one eats one's newfound friends.'

'I wouldn't know,' I said. 'But thanks.' I held my

head in that still, quiet way that is necessary to properly listen for something, except I couldn't actually hear it with my ears. It was more like a full-body hearing, if you know what I mean. It was in the sea but it was older than the mountains. Ancient as the dinosaurs. And ready to have babies.

'Archie,' I said, 'can you feel that?'

'The hum of the fly?'

'No, the big thing. In the ocean. Coming.'

Archie was still and quiet too, for a second. 'I can. Good Lord! But why is she coming *here*?'

Of course – it was a she!

'I really don't know,' I replied. 'But how exciting! She's a day or two away now – wouldn't you agree?'

'More or less, yes.'

'I'm so ready for this, my whole body is vibrating.'

'I'd rather you didn't come near my web, in that case,' Archie said.

I was impatient and jiggedy, and Archie wanted to sleep. I had to DO something, so to pass the time, I decided to take Cornelius back.

A while ago, I'd spooned some frogspawn into a cup to watch the tadpoles grow in a tank in my room (and teach them some nouns in French). This fella was ready to go back home. 'Least that's what he reckoned. I was taking him to the estuary, and Rufus was coming with me for a change of scenery.

It was around eight-thirty in the evening, so it was still light, but a bit cooler, and my shadow was long, like a mummy-long-legs. I'd wet my hands so it would be pleasant for Cornelius, and I was telling him about not liking the courgette bits of vegetable lasagne (not relevant) with Rufus ambling happily behind.

I nearly jumped when I saw Nathaniel sitting on the grass near the edge of the marshes, his bike on the ground by his side.

'What d'you have there?' he asked, getting up. 'Let me guess. *Rana temporaria.*'

I ignored him. I would have turned around and gone back home again, but Cornelius was excited and I didn't want to disappoint him. He was just a baby, really. Plus, I had to prove my trustworthiness as an animal warrior to the big mamma on her way. I carried on walking and Nathaniel followed, even though I had wellies on and he didn't and his shoes were now completely submerged in the swampy mush by the verge of the estuary.

'Latin name,' he added. 'For the common frog.'

'Go away,' I said. I whispered to Cornelius through my fingers, 'Nearly there. You take care, now. I'll miss you.' I bent down by the riverbank, found some strong reeds to hold on to, then bent lower, opening my hands. Cornelius and I smiled at each other. He paused for a moment, unable to believe the moment had finally arrived, thanked me (silently, of course) and jumped off my palm shouting *Rivière! Soleil! Mouches! Grenouilles!* (He remembered! Which just goes to show that it's always worth teaching frogs French nouns whenever you can.)

I wiped my hands on my shirt and watched him go. He was so tiny, even though he *thought* he was big now. I felt like his mother watching him go off on his own for the first time – full of concern and fear for his safety. *Take care, little fella*, I thought.

'Common frogs have many predators,' Nathaniel said, looking at the ripple Cornelius had just made. 'Birds of prey, crows, gulls, herons, stoats, weasels, otters—'

I whipped around in horror. '*Shh!*'

'Snakes—'

'*I said shh!*'

'Most are killed by cars, though.'

'*What's the matter with you? He'll hear you!*'

Nathaniel stopped talking. He just sat there on that bank of sand and watched the river flow. I couldn't see Cornelius, but in my head I suggested he stay away from roads and wished him well, wherever he was.

Then I started walking home in a mood with Nathaniel. Frightening a baby frog should be a criminal offence. Rufus shuffled behind and Nathaniel did too, his shoes squelching as he walked. 'Pacman frogs in South America have huge mouths,' he said, 'which is how they got their name. You know, like the video game.'

I didn't know. I don't have video games in my house. We don't even have a video. I kept walking.

'One species of horned Pacman in Argentina eats anything that moves near its mouth: insects, lizards, rodents, even other frogs. They can suffocate trying to swallow prey that's too big.'

I shook my head. I couldn't help it. Partly because that was shocking and partly because he'd scared Cornelius (and me too, to be honest) and was still there talking to me when I was clearly unhappy about that.

'Goliath frogs in Africa grow to the size of small dogs. My favourite are glass frogs, though. They're as small as a fingernail, with transparent skin so you can see their insides.'

Annoyed as I was, my mind flashed with questions. Were they also from Africa? Whose fingernail – an adult's or a child's? *Transparent skin?* Nathaniel wheeled his bike beside me, and as I passed the house with the broken boat and the horse box at the side, I turned to face him. 'What do you want?'

'Sorry if I was tactless. About your frog. I didn't mean to—'

'Yes, you did.'

'I just . . . thought that if—' He pushed his hand through his hair. 'I don't know what to say most of the time. I get it wrong.'

I put my hands on my hips over Daddy Jeremy's big shirt. 'You don't say. You came to find me to tell me that?'

'Yes. And to say that . . . I didn't know about you, and . . . and now I do.'

My skin prickled. What exactly did he know? By then we'd reached our gate. 'Great. Bye, then. Good luck and everything,' I said. 'Rufus, come.'

But Rufus didn't come. His hairy chin was resting at the side of Nathaniel's knee and he was enjoying the head stroke.

Rufus. I glared at him. *Are you coming or what?*

Rufus said, *Mmmm. Earrrr ruuubbb. Feels niiiice.*

'Rufus knows he can trust me,' Nathaniel said. 'And you can, too.'

I jutted out my chin. *Rufus. Come.*

'He was hurt, wasn't he?' Nathaniel continued, looking into Rufus's eyes. 'By bad people.'

I started scratching my arm. Hard.

'They were cruel to him.' Nathaniel's eyes stayed on Rufus, even though Rufus got flooded with sad, and looked to the side. 'So he was taken away, and Mr and Mrs Goddard gave him a home.'

My skin prickled all over my body but I stopped scratching my arm because I loved Daddy Jeremy and he'd asked me not to.

'And that's what happened to you, too, wasn't it, Ivy?'

The world came crashing down on my head, like Chicken Licken in the story Aisling had read to me when I was small.

'Stop talking,' I whispered. 'Stay away from me.'

And I walked up the path with Rufus plodding silently behind me.

34. NATHANIEL

I stood there a while, staring silently at her yellow door, hoping she might open it again. But she didn't. Eventually, I turned around and walked back to my mother's house, wondering how I'd ever get through life. Emotions are an entire area I know nothing about. Girls, too. Where and how would I learn to say the right thing to the right person at the right time?

It was twilight by then. My mother was standing by the back door in her kaftan and yellow rubber gloves. She had a smudgy smear across her forehead and her hair in a loose bun.

'Oh dear. Everything all right?' she asked.

'No.'

'Can I help?' I didn't answer, so she asked, 'Midnight feast? Would you like one, I mean. A midnight feast.'

'It's not midnight.'

'Minor detail.' She walked into the kitchen and I followed. 'I have the bread you like, cheese from Jim's cows, and chocolate biscuits. Feast or no feast?'

My brain hurt but I was hungry so I said, 'Feast.'

Now, I know lots about other creatures' brains but not an awful lot about my own.

I know that the brains of the world's smallest spiders are so large compared to the rest of their bodies, they spill out of their heads and down their legs.

I know that octopus's brains have 65 million neurons that connect to their arms, which each have half a million neurons, so their arms can think independently to their main brain. That's why a shrimp can be handed from sucker to sucker towards its mouth and a severed arm can crawl on its own and pick up food.

My favourite brain fact, though, is that there's a species of parasitic fungus that can turn ants into zombies. It feeds on the ant's organs and extends filaments into its brain, making it climb to the top of nearby plants. Then the fungus kills the ant and sprouts from its head as a mushroom.

But my brain? It's different. It doesn't work like other people's. As if it were wired in another way and driven by something else. Hopefully not parasitic fungi, but who knows?

'I want to go to Charles and Nancy's earlier than arranged,' I said, pushing my glasses up my nose. They needed tightening but I was waiting until I reached Aunt Nancy's. My mother rarely changed out of her kaftan and I would have felt extremely uncomfortable about her wearing that at the optician's. 'Preferably tomorrow.'

She was taking the cheese out of the fridge, but she stopped and turned around. 'What? Why?'

'This house is a mess. The way you speak confuses me. And you aren't truthful about what happened, so I don't trust you.'

Her shoulders slumped. She closed the fridge door and sat down opposite me, looking at me so hard I felt agitated, even though I kept my gaze on the wall.

'Nathaniel, this house isn't a mess because I'm messy. It's a mess because I'm clearing it out so it *won't* be messy. My father and his brother were dreadful hoarders – there's a great deal to sift through and I want to give these things to people who might need them, not just throw them away, and that takes time. So many people are less fortunate and we should do all we can to help them. I started to clear the house out when I moved in, but then Grandma got sick and I didn't have much time before you arrived.'

'OK.' I kept my eyes on the wall. It was painted

pale yellow and there was a hairline crack between the window and the cupboard.

'As for . . . I *am* speaking more slowly. Haven't you noticed?'

I hadn't noticed.

'My head, you see. Works too quickly for my mouth. I'm *trying* to slow down and make sense – the last thing I want to do is confuse you. Order.' She held her forefinger in the air and corrected herself. 'I know you need peace and order,' she said, more deliberately, 'and I'm clearing out so you have that. I very much want this to be your home – a place you'll love and want to spend time in. Perhaps even . . . live in. Permanently. If . . . you should want.'

I didn't want. Above the crack in the wall was a photograph of Grandma holding me when I was a baby in her sitting room. I was in a blue vest with popper buttons, and I was crying. She didn't seem worried. Grandma was like that. She was composed and unruffled, and she always did the right thing.

'I can't live with someone who doesn't tell the truth,' I said, and with my eyes on the photograph, I summoned the courage to add, 'or with a mother who didn't want me.'

Her hand covered her mouth and her face crumpled – I could see it in the periphery of my vision. I glanced sideways at her after a while. She seemed in great pain but I wasn't sure why. Emotions are strange. I just don't understand them. After a minute or two, she took her hand off her mouth and whispered, 'I always wanted you.'

I stiffened. 'OK.'

'Always, Nathaniel.'

'OK.' I stood up, pushing my chair back. 'Then why did I grow up with Grandma and never see you? I don't feel hungry now. I'm going to bed.'

35. IVY

After dinner, and long after bedtime and moonrise, I slid out of my window. I was still fuming about Nathaniel poking his nose in my business – and Rufus's as well, for that matter – but I couldn't spend all night bellowing like a deer having birthday ribbons tied around its antlers (not relevant). Because it was time.

She was almost here.

It was very late by then, and by late, I mean like eleven or eleven-thirty at night, because it gets dark at around ten-thirty in June. I am not allowed out that late, and I am absolutely not allowed to climb out of my bedroom window on to the porch roof and shimmy down the drainpipe. I've had to do it a couple of times before, when I heard a bat in trouble or a pig was giving birth, but this was different. She was calling me. She needed love and care and protection, and I was the only one who could help, mainly because I was the only one who could understand her and knew she was coming.

This was the most important mission of my entire life and I couldn't get it wrong.

I didn't need humans, not ever – it was just me and animals for evermore and we'd be totally fine as long as we had each other and that made my heart dance like in ballet when the tiny, bendy woman gets launched into the air by the man in yellow tights and it looks like she's flying.

I crept to the front of the house, feeling guilty. I'd promised Jeremy and Aisling I would keep a low profile and here I was, sneaking out of the house on my own at night to go down to the beach to meet a giant creature who was a long way from home hoping to do something very unusual on our beach. But if I kept a very, very low profile and helped her all by myself, no one would know (except the entire animal kingdom, obviously) and I'd keep my promise to my foster parents. And keep my home and the harmony of our world (my human family's and my animal family's).

I opened the front door for Rufus (he's not great at climbing down drainpipes), mouthed 'sorry' to Jeremy and Aisling (well, actually to the staircase, but it was aimed at them in bed) and closed the front door as quietly as I could.

Rufus and I could see really well because the moon was full and bright. The cars, the houses, the grass, the foxes, the drifty clouds and the church steeple of St Edmund's were almost as clear as they were in daylight, just with a bluish tinge. I love that in moonlight, it's bright enough to juggle stones on the beach and catch owls having flirty romances in trees, but I don't like that moonlight strips all the greens away because it feels a bit disrespectful to the trees, and that's just crazy because the trees deserve the most respect of anything on this planet. When the sun comes out and lights the world up again, I cheer for the plants and the trees in a huge celebration of the colour green, and so do all the birds. (If you think they're singing, I'm sorry but you've got that a little bit wrong.)

Rufus looked at me. *Come on*, he said. He could feel her coming too.

Coming, Daddy Rufus, I said, and we ran off.

The air was still warm and fuzzy. The day had been melt-your-head hot again, and because England was pretending to be Spain, the jellyfish were still visiting. Martin was filled with giant plastic-bag lookalikes that shimmered in the moonlight. I knew they were jellyfish, obviously, because I am at one with the world and the creatures and can tell the difference between a carrier bag and a jellyfish, plus carrier bags aren't that big unless you buy a minivan and need a plastic bag to carry it home in.

I wonder whether Mother Nature meant to make jellyfish look like floating plastic bags. I don't know why she'd do that. Or maybe when people invented plastic bags, they thought about what they'd look like in the water and evilly modelled them on jellyfish. Humans can be shockingly cruel. Either way, it's bad news for anything that eats jellyfish.

Although I was very not-allowed-out, the dunes opposite our house are on the wide, open stretch of beach, and with Rufus and the broad sea and the bright moonlight, I felt safe and happy. All the photo-taking tourists had walked their dogs and eaten their fish and chips and gone to the pub to drink local ale and played bridge and whatever else adults do in the evenings, so it was just Rufus and me and nature and the animal kingdom as far as the eye could see, and believe me, they made it as busy as any city centre.

I scanned the surface of the sea and my blood fizzled with excitement. Rufus and I ran down to the shore, checking as we did whether the jellyfish glowed in the moonlight because you'd think so, right? I wanted to sing them a song in Jellyfishese because it's important to welcome strangers and make them feel at home. Then I'd help her – the turtle, if she was a turtle, which I was pretty sure she was – in any way I could and go straight home before anyone discovered I was out of bed.

Clouds passed over the moon, giving it a ghostly halo. Martin was hooshing and kooshing happily and I was happy too (but without making hooshing and kooshing noises).

Daddy Rufus and I sat on the beach, singing. Well, I was singing. Rufus sometimes hums along, but that night he was too excited. Jellyfish aren't the most beautiful or interesting sea creatures, but those ones were pretty amazing. Giant barrel jellyfish really are enormous – as big as tents – *bigger* than tents. Well, bigger than *my* tent, but then it's only a two-man and those men would have to be very small and like sleeping with their elbows in each other's faces.

Hundreds of jellyfish rippled and blobbed near the surface, and any teacher that tells you that 'blob' isn't a verb hasn't been around enough jellyfish. As they blobbed, disappeared under a wave and then blobbed gently up again, I sang them a song about how lovely it was to be see-through and blobby with pink coral tentacles and no bones (I made it up: it wasn't a song you'd know) and then, just as I got to the chorus about tentacles being better than arms because then you can give hundreds of hugs at once, something heart-stopping caught my eye.

I stopped singing, stood up and walked right to the water's edge, my wellies inside the waves and Rufus behind me on the damp sand.

I stared at Martin. The hyperactive fish, and the shocked shells and molluscs, almost swore with astonishment but then substituted the swear words with cleaner ones because children (i.e. me) were around. None of them had seen anything like this here before and we were all mega-excited.

And then I frowned. What *was* that? Did I just see—? Was that her? Or was it a giant, flat piece of leather? Or a huge piece of wet wood dotted with mouldy white marks? Or a leather Viking shield? Was it a suitcase? Uh-uh. Way too big for that. Part of a ship? A raft?

All my hairs on my arms were up, and half of the ones on my head (and my hair is LONG).

Whatever it was, I couldn't see it any more.

I finished my jellyfish song, but in a louder voice, because with so many of them in there, the ones at the back couldn't hear me. Then I watched the water, wondering. Moonlight is a tricky, playful thing.

Martin swelled and kished. My eyes scanned the heaving mass of sea. The far horizon was dotted with lights from the fishing trawlers and spies watching me with binoculars from their ships (probably). Jellyfish fluttered and blobbed, and the moon blasted out its spooky, horror-film light. I stood as still as a post, but one with long hair and a dog daddy behind me.

Whatever it was rose again, making my whole chest lift. It was the size of the roof of a car, but oval and ridged, going to a point at the back. And then a flipper flipped, causing the water to ripple and splash.

I gasped.

Rufus barked.

And there she was. A head the size of a football emerged from Martin, and my heart stopped.

I was face to face with an enormous – and I mean enormous – turtle.

She held her head up and looked at me, and I looked at her, and we *zshoomed* into each other.

She showed me eggs. Lots of them. And I mean lots.

I opened my eyes wide and she ducked under the surface, her enormous back curving down behind her. Rufus barked again, so I grabbed his collar.

Rufus! I was right! A turtle! Here! On our beach! She's come to lay her eggs.

Rufus barked, *What's a turtle? Why is she here? She smells funny. I'm telling Clyde! CLYDE! CLYDE! GET DOWN HERE AND SMELL THIS!*

NO! I said sternly. *Daddy Rufus, stop. Clyde can't hear you from here, and you'll scare her away!*

He stopped barking. He's good like that.

We watched in silence near the shoreline, waiting to see if she surfaced again. We waited. And waited. I kept staring at Martin. He stared back (he always wins staring competitions). A cow gave birth to quadruplets in Texas. Lemurs ran from a hyena in Madagascar. The world rotated so it became dark in Saudi Arabia, and light in whatever country is opposite Saudi Arabia.

Worried she'd gone, I cleared my throat and sang some more. It was a jellyfish song, but I didn't know any about turtles and I was too nervous to make any up. She seemed to like the jellyfish one, anyway. I finished the first verse and the water flickered again. Then the huge, dark, monstrous shape moved slowly towards me.

I walked backwards, holding my breath (and Rufus's collar) and stood to one side. My heart pumped in loud thumpy thuds, but I kept musical-statues-still and told Rufus to stop going *grrr*.

She emerged from the water like a giant, flat monster, then hauled herself on to the sand.

I stood to one side. She was so big. I'd never seen a creature as big as that. Not ever. And although I knew she was gentle and harmless, she was also enormous, and that's pretty scary.

We stood quietly for a long while – Rufus, me and her – a little freaked out but enjoying being with each other on the beach in the moonlight.

Then slowly, very slowly, she flapped, juddered and shimmied her massive body away from us towards the dunes, leaving tractor-like tracks in the sand that caught in notches in the moonlight. Rufus and I tiptoed behind her, quietly, keeping quite far away, just in case.

Just past the first tuft of long grass, in a circular spot of the dunes that seemed safe and protected, she stopped to rest. I lay flat behind a dune tuft nearby, holding Rufus's collar.

The turtle brought her front flippers forwards like wings, chopped them into the sand to make a well, and sat there.

I thought it was a good moment to welcome her, so in my head, I said, *I'm so happy you came. I was worried you wouldn't, after . . . you know.*

I winced.

I haven't been so . . .

Ivy, so good to meet you at long, long last, she said in a lilting, rolling accent. Then she sent me an invisible hug of turtle love that filled me up until I sighed. *Don't you worry, Ivy,* she went on. *You do everything you can, and that is marvellous. We appreciate it all.*

I felt like crying with joy. With my heart bursting, I stroked Rufus and he agreed, saying, *We do. It's true.*

I smiled and kissed his nose, which tasted salty and stuck sand on my lips.

We watched the turtle. After a while, she started shovelling sand with her rear flippers, one after the other, so it sprayed up behind her. Then she rested, her throat pumping, and did it again.

She sat doing that for ages as she laid some of her eggs. Rufus sat with me and didn't bark, mainly because I told him Clyde preferred poodle butts to turtles any day. Then she slammed her flippers down again and again, covering the well with sand. After what seemed like hours, she turned and hauled herself back across the beach.

Rufus and I crept along behind her. She reached the breaking waves, paused a second or two, and slipped into the sea.

Rufus and I stayed crouched on the sand, breathing in hard raspy breaths. I kept my eyes on Martin, in awe and a little overwhelmed. Not only because the jelly-fish in there were about to be munched like Haribos,

214

but because I had just witnessed a miracle of nature.

A giant turtle had laid her eggs on the beach right in front of me. And I was the only human in the whole world who knew about it.

Rufus barked, and I realized what he was telling me.

We had a job to do. We had to make sure no one disturbed those eggs. That was why the mother sent the eggy message into my brain: she was taking on the services of Ivy Pink Floyd's Animal Action Agency.

I had my first real (non-human) case!

I was happier than I'd ever been before, and that's saying something when you've seen a butterfly break through its cocoon or a lost ant find its trail again.

I had to protect those babies with my life.

The only problem was, I didn't know how.

36. NATHANIEL

I didn't know if it was a good thing or a bad thing that all my important belongings fitted into a cabin suitcase and a backpack. Perhaps I didn't have a very exciting life. Or perhaps I didn't need much to make me happy. I folded and packed my clothes, slotted the book on climate change, my spare rubber balls and my Papermate pens into my backpack, and lay on the bed.

In the morning, I would leave this house, my mother and Southwold without making a single friend or finding whatever it was that was here for me. Unless . . .

I could hear my mother talking to Lola in the kitchen, so I crossed the hallway as silently as I could, and opened the door to her bedroom. The floor space was filled with ornaments and lampshades and wooden chests and rolled-up rugs and so many things, I had to count to ten in all the languages I knew *and* two invented ones to calm down.

I put one foot in front of another very slowly, so the floorboards wouldn't creak, in the direction of her desk near the window. A pile of papers sat to one side, so I picked them up: they were utility bills, bank statements and letters from the hospital about Grandma. Underneath a few cards of condolence, I saw an envelope with Grandma's writing on the front and stopped still.

Grandma's letter to my mother.

I listened for noises downstairs. My mother's voice was still faintly audible, then I heard Lola screech noisily. I picked up the envelope. I was conflicted about reading it because it was private. It wasn't addressed to or meant for me. Reading it was wrong.

I put it back and turned to leave, but then hesitated.

I wanted to know the truth, and the truth was in that envelope. No one had ever explained to me why Grandma had brought me up, or what had happened between her and my mother, and if I didn't read it, I might never know.

I lifted the papers and picked up the envelope again. What if the truth was awful? What if it were something I really couldn't keep to myself, and then my mother would know I'd read a private letter that was none of my business and I had no right to read?

I slid the letter out of the envelope. It was two pages long with writing on both sides. I skimmed over it. On the first page and a half, Grandma reminisced about what kind of child my mother had been (wayward and free-spirited), and recounted fond memories of Christmases and birthdays. She moved on to my mother being a difficult, headstrong teen, and then there was this:

As I sit propped in my hospital bed, looking out on to the pleasant spring garden, you are in my thoughts. I deeply regret that we spent all those years apart, Henrietta. Yes, you were selfish and silly and did reckless things, but you were young, and when all is said and done, you are my daughter and I did not treat you fairly. After what you did in Mexico, I considered you unfit to look after yourself, never mind a child. You always abandoned all your responsibilities and I was not going to allow you to abandon him as well. Nathaniel is different, special, and I was adamant that he was better off with me than with a mother like you. But he is your son, and I was wrong to have taken him from you. I understand why you left for India after I filed for custody of him. I assumed at the time that you were running away from your responsibilities yet again, and that you didn't care about him, but I know now that you left because you did care – very much so – and my taking him from you hurt you more than you could bear.

I profusely apologize. I can never give you back the years you should have spent with your son but I hope – and have every faith – that you and he will find each other and love each other. I hope that one day you will be able to forgive me for what I've done, as I have forgiven you. I was not the mother I should have been or that you needed, and for that I am truly, truly sorry.

I have always and will always love you,

Mummy

I stood for a minute in silence, then folded the letter, slid it back into the envelope and returned to my room.

Through the open window, I could hear the fizzle of the waves, and see the bright, full moon. I lay on my bed with the sheet covering my nose, even though it was a hot, humid night. Tears leaked from my eyes on to the pillow. Good job Uncle Charles couldn't see me.

My grandmother wasn't who I thought she was, and I didn't know my mother at all. I didn't know myself, either. I didn't know why I disliked mess or loud noises, or why I only ate specific food or why telling people animal facts made me feel better when I was uncomfortable. But perhaps Ivy was right and those were the reasons I had such trouble making friends.

My insides gripped tightly as if an anaconda was squeezing them (and they squeeze at 90 psi, which is 9,000 pounds of pressure per square inch, which is very very hard).

Perhaps Ivy was right about something else, too: maybe humans really *were* terrible and best avoided. I'd wanted to communicate with them better so we could work together to save the world, but now I didn't trust anyone at all. I hadn't discovered what was here for me, hadn't made a single friend or bonded with a single animal, and tomorrow I would leave. Colin would drive me to Darsham Station, where

Rory would meet me to chaperone me to London and no doubt ignore me all the way. Uncle Charles would meet me at Liverpool Street, and possibly Aunt Nancy if she'd finished surgery by then, and we'd board a train to Sussex. Then, at the end of the holidays, I'd return to boarding school, where I had no friends, and that would be that.

Feeling all hope was lost for myself and my planet, I stared at the moonlit sky with my eyelids getting heavier and heavier until I fell asleep.

37. IVY

If I'd been asleep I'd have missed all this. Sometimes answering the call of nature by scrambling down from your bedroom window is the very best thing to do. Usually it isn't, mind you, because causing rumpuses with caring foster parents is always best avoided, and children out at night with their dogs are not usually safe (so don't copy me).

But this was a rare and special exception.

After the turtle juddered back into the sea, I realized we had a problem. A big one. How could I protect her eggs all by myself?

I needed to pee and eat and sleep and go to school, so I couldn't be here twenty-four hours a day.

I couldn't even stay here all of tonight protecting them, because it was already super late and I wasn't allowed out at night in the first place.

I bit my lip.

Rufus, I said, my face going as white as the moon. *What do we do?*

Rufus looked at the eggs. *Tasty*, he said, in a voice very much like Scooby Doo's.

I gasped. *Rufus, how **could** you?*

And then I panicked. Early in the morning, people would turn up to walk their dogs. Later, others would lie on the beach sunbathing, have barbecues on the dunes, throw Frisbees, scrape surfboards across the sand, dig holes and tunnels to bury their family members, and stomp around about playing with footballs and kicking sand in people's faces.

Those eggs were in danger.

This task was too big and important for Ivy Pink Floyd's Animal Action Agency to handle all by itself, especially as I had only just set it up and had no idea what I was doing. Protecting those eggs – like protecting every living creature – was a positive (and almost definitely the most important) step in saving the world, and that was what my agency was all about.

But I couldn't do it alone. And animals couldn't help me. Not with this.

Rufus, I said. *Nathaniel was right. I do need humans. Some things you just can't do alone, and saving the world and its beautiful creatures is one of them.*

Hmm, said Rufus. Sounding *again* like Scooby Doo.

Rufus, I bet in Jamaica and Mexico and wherever, turtles can nest and survive, but this is Southwold and we are not prepared for this. I looked at the area of sand where her eggs lay, and gulped. I was one person and I was only eleven and this was a bit too important to be in the hands of someone clueless, which is a big realization to have when you're in a panic.

Mother Turtle, I'll be back, I said, and – grabbing Rufus's collar, just in case – I ran as fast as I could to Huntington House.

I reached it without seeing a headless ghost, which pleased me no end. Still, the house was deathly dark. I didn't know which room Nathaniel slept in, so I couldn't throw stones at his window or climb a drain-pipe to wake him, like they do in books – I had to knock on the front door. Henny opened it after the fifth series of machine-gun knocks, with fright in her eyes and a weird sheet-dress on.

'Ivy! What is it?' she asked, her eyes searching as if a crisis was standing behind me disguised as dark air.

'I need to talk to Nathaniel!' I said, puffing. Look, it's a fair run from the dunes, and can I remind you – *ghosts*?

'It's the middle of the night. Is it an emergency?' she asked. A small plait of hair lay like the tail of a sleeping creature over her shoulder.

'It is,' I replied, trying to catch my breath. 'It really is.'

She let me in, told me to wait in the parlour and went up to get him.

Their parlour was even creepier than Gun Hill. I kept thinking there was a ghost in the corner that wanted to kill me, but I couldn't see one. I sure could feel it, though. I'm not scared of spiders, snakes, creepy-crawlies, vampires, werewolves or people like Gus who jump out at me in graveyards shouting 'Woooh!' (not relevant), but ghosts? I've never seen one, but you can feel them in rooms, as cold as midwinter draughts under doors. The air has a lingering chill, and it makes me stiffen like Jeremy does when you give him a hug.

I was very happy to hear footsteps coming down the stairs.

But they weren't his. They were hers. 'Ivy, I'm terribly sorry but he doesn't want to see you. He's been feeling rather ... low and he has an early start in the morning.'

'But ... it's an emergency.'

'Has somebody died?'

'Not yet,' I said, 'but they will if we don't do something.'

'Oh, dear. Anyone I know?' she asked.

'It's unlikely to be anyone human,' Nathaniel said.

He stood at the door, looking sleepy. His voice was groggy and his hair was standing up and curling over like a breaking wave, only dark brown and soundless. I must say, you never know what kind of pyjamas people wear unless you have sleepovers with them, and you never have sleepovers with boys. I was surprised to see his were short-sleeved, striped and matching, which seemed a bit smart for bed – especially in the heat – but at least he wasn't wearing his anorak.

Henny said, 'Ivy, does Jeremy know you're out?'

I shook my head. 'And I'd really rather he didn't.'

'Well, he must, I'm afraid. I'll call and tell him you're with me.' And she walked up the creaky stairs, which made me look in the corner again, just to check.

I turned to Nathaniel. 'Big huge serious emergency. I need your help.'

'Why?' He scrunched his nose up so his nostrils looked like the dots of two rhetorical questions.

'Because she came! To the beach. Just now.'

'I mean, why are you telling *me*?'

'Please don't ask questions!' I said, getting panicky. 'Just come quick. I can't leave them on their own.'

'You said you didn't want to be friends with me.'

I was trying to think of a good comeback, because

I did say that, but then a cockerel crowed. Daddy Jeremy's cockerel used to crow all through the night and drive him mad. He gave the cockerel to Jim in the end in return for half a dozen eggs once a week. Jim's hens' eggs have the yellowest, creamiest yolks you've ever seen, which is totally relevant because those eggs give me my protein and without it, I wouldn't have had the energy to run like a maniac across Gun Hill in the dark.

'It's after midnight,' Nathaniel said, looking yawny. 'I have a long journey tomorrow.'

My heart lurched. '*Journey?* You can't leave!' I cried. 'They need us!'

He didn't answer. I think he was still asleep, really, just with his eyes open.

38. NATHANIEL

I wanted to go back to sleep. I didn't know why she had come and I wasn't interested in playing her game, but she carried on regardless.

'Don't you see?' she asked with a choked voice. 'This is what my gift is all about! If I can't save lives, then there's no point.'

I sighed. 'What gift?'

Ivy put her hands on her waist, gathering her huge shirt in, and said, 'I can understand animals and they can understand me.'

'No, you can't.'

'Do you think I'm making it up? Everyone can do it. It's easy.'

'*I* can't.'

'You could if you stopped being such a logical scientist. You're wasting time! We need to go!'

I didn't have a rubber ball on me and very much

wanted to be elsewhere, preferably somewhere quiet. 'The only place I'm going is to bed.'

'Fine,' Ivy said, throwing her hands in the air. 'Fine. If you think sleep is more important than helping one of the most amazing creatures on Earth, then go back upstairs.'

I turned to go back upstairs. Obviously, I'd have helped if one of the most amazing creatures on Earth needed it, but this was probably a piglet that wanted to try wearing socks or a gerbil with anger management issues. The stairs were dark, but the light from the sitting-room lamp cast a triangular glow across a mandala painting of a demon face surrounded by concentric circles. I didn't like it and looked away.

'Don't go! You're right,' Ivy blurted.

'About what?' I stopped walking and stood at the foot of the staircase in the shadows.

'I can't save the world all by myself. Most of the time, I can't even save the animals I meet. And I have to.' She started crying, which made me feel rather uncomfortable, and repeated, 'I have to.'

I leant against the banister. I was tired, and standing up was wearisome. I didn't understand why she was upset, but then she explained.

'When I was small,' Ivy said, her voice travelling easily through the quiet of the house, 'my mum didn't pick me up from nursery one day. Everyone else went home, but no one came for me. My teacher phoned and phoned and phoned but there was no reply. Eventually, my dad answered but when my teacher came off the phone, she said Daddy wasn't in a fit state to look after me and I had to go home with her.'

I stood listening in the dark hallway. My mother came out of her room. She heard Ivy speaking and put her finger against her lips to indicate that I should keep quiet. She stood still, presumably so the floor wouldn't creak, and I turned my attention back to Ivy.

She was standing in the middle of the room in the lamplight, scratching her arm.

'That teacher scared me,' Ivy continued, 'and so did her house. I cried all night on my own in the dark. The next day, my dad came to collect me. He said my mummy had gone back to her country and I'd never see her again.' She paused, then added in a low voice, 'He was horrible to me before but he was even worse after that. He got drunk a lot, and when I cried because I was hungry, he locked me in my room.'

My mother looked down at me and I looked up at her but neither of us spoke. The last time I saw my father, I was five and a half. I felt very uneasy with him because he had long hair, and he kept trying to hug me and hold my hand. I refused to see him after that, but he seemed quite tame compared to Ivy's father. Perhaps I'd misjudged him.

'That's why I give animals food and make sure someone cares for them and loves them,' Ivy said, her voice trailing to a whisper. 'Because when I was small and I needed love, nobody cared for me.'

My mother's arm crossed her stomach and her other hand covered her mouth.

I entered the doorway of the parlour and faced Ivy.

She let go of the arm she'd been scratching, wiped her eyes with her sleeve, and said sniffing, 'You're . . . the only human friend I have, Nathaniel. And I . . . really, really need your help. Please come with me. I can't let them down . . . I just can't.'

I nodded, cleared my throat and said, 'I'll get dressed.'

39. IVY

I stood wondering why we say 'get dressed' when men don't wear dresses. It makes no sense. And telling him my life story was not something I had planned to do. Not then, and not ever. Eileen, my social worker, said I never needed to tell anyone anything, not unless I wanted to. Daddy Jeremy and Aisling knew, of course. Otherwise it was nobody's business.

But I was desperate, and because I really did need Nathaniel to help me, it just came out.

He didn't ask a million more questions, or look at me with kind, sorry eyebrows, or shake his head at how awful it was, or do any of the things adults did when they heard about it, and that made it easier. And he really was quick at getting trousered and anoraked, which I was grateful for.

When he came down, Henny was with him. She

was dressed too. She grabbed a shawl from the edge of the sofa and said, 'No responsible mother could let you two go out alone in the middle of the night. Besides, it sounds exciting.'

'We need to be quick,' I said, more worried than I'd ever been in my life.

I was so grateful when they started running. For the record, you can't run fast in wellies. They might be great for wading but they're rubbish when lives are endangered and you need to sprint.

Rufus ran behind us, his ears flapping in the wind. The air was alive and full of mischief. Bats flew low in circles and small creatures rustled in the grass. An owl hooted, making the spooky-scale rise by about a trillion per cent. I ran on, trying to be fearless, telling owls off for hooting and scaring girls near haunted cannons who shouldn't have been out that late.

'The collective noun is *a parliament of owls*,' Nathaniel said, hearing the hoot, too. It was comforting to know that even in a crisis, he'd come out with a random animal fact.

'It'd be a *horror film of owls* if I had my way,' I yelled, making sure the owls heard me.

When we reached the dunes, I fell on my hands and knees and checked the area. It seemed fine, so I started building a sandcastle barrier, not *on* the eggs, but in front of them and round the back. Nathaniel switched the torch on and held it up, watching me, as Henny looked around, frowning in confusion.

'So this is the emergency?' Nathaniel grumbled. 'Making sandcastles?'

'Actually, we need crates! Sandcastles won't be strong enough. They'll do for now, but . . . we need to build a barrier like the Great Wall of China!'

'To protect the *sandcastles*?'

'To protect the *babies*!'

'What babies?' Henny asked.

Nathaniel was still being grumpy. 'You woke me up in the middle of the night,' he said. 'The least you can do is tell me what you're talking about.'

My stomach dropped. 'I can't cause a rumpus. I really can't. But I can't let them die, either.'

'The sandcastles?' he said.

'Let who die?' Henny asked.

'THE TURTLES!' I bawled.

They both gasped. To be honest, their reaction was more intense than I thought it would be. Maybe I should have mentioned it before.

'What turtles?' Henny yelled.

'These ones!' I pointed to the sand and added, 'There are eggs under here. Lots of them. A huge turtle came out of Martin earlier and—'

'Martin?' Nathaniel asked.

'The sea, the sea! A gigantic leatherback turtle came out of the sea and laid her eggs on the sand. Right here.'

'*Leatherback?*' Nathaniel repeated. He'd turned into a parrot again. He stood beside me like a giant shocked donkey (not relevant) but before I could say anything more, Henny scanned the sand and said, 'Ivy, where's the nest? Where exactly are they?'

I burst into tears and hugged Henny hard.

She believed me.

'There,' I said, pointing to the area of sand. 'I'm trying to protect them by blocking off this part of the beach, but sandcastles won't work. Even crates won't—' but then I stopped because Nathaniel burst into tears.

I stared at him with wide eyes. I'd never seen a boy cry. I'd seen girls cry, like when I fell on to Sadie Cleaver's doll's house (not relevant) but I didn't think boys even *could*, you know, biologically. What had upset him? The turtles? The *sandcastles*? The fact that I'd hugged his mother?

'Um ... are you OK?' I asked. I kind of needed him to hurry up with his inner crisis and start helping. His tears shone in the moonlight. What went on in that brainy head of his? Apart from random facts and his love of spit, it was all a big mystery. You could cheer up dogs with a doggie biscuit, and hedgehogs with knock-knock jokes, but boys? When *their* troubles can be solved with a doggie biscuit, there'll be hope for the world.

'Turtles,' he said. I thought he was going to tell me a random fact about them but after a pause, he went on. 'Grandma and I were planning a trip to see them, but then—' He wiped his nose with his finger. 'I want to believe you, Ivy, but turtles don't—'

'UUURGGHH!'

WHY DID NO ONE EVER BELIEVE ME?

40. NATHANIEL

My mother seemed to believe her, but what Ivy was saying was impossible.

'Leatherback turtles don't nest in cold European waters,' I persisted. 'They just don't. There are seven species of turtle, and every one nests in warm climates.'

'You believe me, right?' Ivy asked my mother. 'Because it's horrible when no one believes you.'

'Of course,' my mother replied. 'But I'm finding it all a little . . . hard to digest.'

My nose was running. I couldn't wipe it on my sleeve – it would look like a snail trail on my anorak. Snail mucus acts as a lubricant to reduce friction against the surface on which they pass, and also allows snails to travel upside down. The largest land snail is 38 centimetres, which is bigger than a ruler. And the largest sea snail is 90 centimetres, which is like three rulers, and weighs 18 kilos. Which is an interesting fact, but it didn't seem the right time to say so. 'There can't be any eggs,' I insisted.

'Well, there are,' Ivy said darkly.

My mother said, 'Sandcastles are pointless, Ivy. The eggs need proper protection.'

I shook my head in exasperation. 'Leatherback eggs incubate between twenty-four and thirty-one degrees.' Neither of them was listening. 'And the sea needs to be warm enough for the hatchlings to survive.' I looked at the sand and added, 'This has been the longest, hottest summer on record, but still.'

My mother gazed at the moonlit sea and said, 'Is she still in there?'

'Yes,' Ivy replied.

'Leatherbacks nest in tropical climates,' I repeated. 'Costa Rica. French Guiana. The Caribbean. Mexico. Not here.' I stood up, brushed the sand off my trousers, and said, 'Can we go now?'

'Ivy,' my mother said. 'Run and get Tom Rosten.'

'The vet?' Ivy asked. 'In Tittlemouse House?'

My mother clipped her hair up and nodded. 'I need to talk to Nathaniel.'

Ivy nodded. 'You'll watch them?'

'With my life.'

Ivy kicked off her wellies and set off across the

dunes. 'All this running,' she yelled. 'I need trainers!'

'Isn't it dangerous for her to go alone?' I asked, concerned for Ivy's safety because my mother clearly wasn't.

My mother shook her head. 'I can see his front door from here.' She pointed to a row of houses. 'She's in my direct line of vision.' Her attention turned to the sand and she added, 'Utterly astonishing. Nathaniel, I have a confession to make.' And then she looked up at me. I couldn't see any relevance at all to the sand, the vet *or* the confession, until she said, 'Nancy and I took eggs from Mexico. Turtle eggs.'

'I . . . don't understand.'

'Turtles had laid eggs on the beach, and there'd been an oil spill. I was worried the slick would wash up and damage them, but I also thought it would be fun to bring some back to England. Turtle researchers from Florida were camping near us, and they had taken eggs back to the US for research, so I knew they could survive. I asked questions about their incubation and knew it was possible, so I persuaded Nancy to do it with me. When we got home, we incubated them under reptile lamps in the airing cupboard in the spare bedroom. What we didn't realize was that the sea needed to be warm as well – we only found that out once we were home, and by then it was too late. We felt awful. A month later, I met your father, fell in love and ran off with him.'

'But ... the eggs,' I said.

'I was sure they'd die anyway. What I didn't know was that Nancy took care of them after I left. When it was close to hatching time, she carried them down to the dunes, buried them in the sand and protected them, just in case they hatched.'

'Is that why she camped there, shooing dogs away?'

'Exactly. Poor Nancy always had to clean up my messes. She said that one hot summer's night, they hatched, and she saw them safely out to sea. I didn't believe her. Nancy was furious with me for abandoning the eggs, and I was certain she was making the hatching up, just to prove a point about how irresponsible I was. Turtles don't nest in Britain, as you well know.'

'But she didn't make it up.'

'Oh, God,' my mother whimpered, shaking her head. 'All those years we didn't talk, and all along ... but why has a turtle come *here* to nest?'

'Most marine turtles,' I explained, happy that I knew this, 'return to the beach where they hatched to lay their eggs. Scientists think they use the Earth's magnetic field to navigate the ocean to find it. And they're only ready to lay eggs fifteen to twenty-five years later.'

'Oh, my gosh!' my mother said, standing up. 'She's one of ours. She's come home to lay her eggs!'

I shook my head. 'Not all marine turtles do that. Olive Ridleys do, green sea turtles do, but leatherbacks don't always.'

'She's one of ours, Nathaniel. She hatched here all those years ago, and somehow she survived. And she's returned to the beach where she was born. Unbelievable! She made it all the way across the ocean to lay her eggs here.'

41. IVY

I might not have run very far, but I made it. By the time I got to the vet's house, my hands were hot and my face felt as purple as a pot of red cabbage that gets knocked from the hob on to the floor by an elbow (not relevant). I'd tell you all about my frantic dash, the fox I saw near the horse box and the pregnant ginger cat on Tom's garage roof, but none of it is relevant. Halfway there, I stepped on sharp gravel and cursed the fact that I hadn't worn different footwear tonight. But when life serves you a plateful of weirdness, you don't stop to get your flip-flops.

I hammered on the tiny door. A dog started barking. A big dog with a big bark that said IF I CATCH YOU I WILL EAT YOU MAKE NO MISTAKE. Then another dog joined in barking ME TOO ME TOO I'LL EAT WHATEVER SCRAPS HE LEAVES BEHIND. I tried to tell them to be calm and shush, but animals – like people – don't always listen.

A blonde woman with a long nightie and a round pregnant belly opened the door, bleary-eyed. I was stressed and scared about the eggs and I hadn't slept and it was dark and it was all a bit overwhelming, to be honest. The dogs barked even louder, and a man's voice shouted at them to stop, so that didn't help with my stress levels, either.

'Are you all right?' the woman asked, her eyes taking in my tangled hair, my filthy no-longer-white shirt and my dirty bare feet. 'It's the middle of the night. Are you on your own?' She held the front of her belly, which worried me. Could babies fall out frontways?

'Is . . . Tom Rosten . . . here?' I asked, panting.

'Is it an emergency?' Her hand was still holding her belly.

'Ye-es,' I said, trying to focus on the emergency and not on her belly. 'It . . . really . . . is.'

'Tom!' she yelled.

The dogs were still deciding quite loudly who'd get which part of me. The house was teeny, like it was made for elves, and a brand-new pram in see-through wrapping stood in the hallway (not relevant). 'Come in,' she said, turning to me. 'He'll be here in a jiffy.'

I shook my head. 'I need to stay where Henny can see me,' I said, and stood at the door for over a minute, which feels like eternity when the eggs of an ancient, endangered creature have just been laid on your beach and your gentle, kind foster parents have asked you not to cause a rumpus so you don't have to leave the only home you've ever felt safe in and your feet hurt from running barefoot and you're standing at a pregnant woman's front door in the middle of the night.

I thought of the eggs and how everyone would rush to protect them if they were *human* babies, which wasn't fair because animals weren't any less important.

'Yes, can I help?' Tom was standing in the doorway, looking really grumpy. (I didn't know how long a jiffy was where they came from, but it wasn't my idea of a jiffy.) He was youngish, dark-haired, and was wearing a black vest and shorts, which wasn't the uniform of an animal warrior, if you ask me. 'Oh. You,' he added. 'No hen tonight?'

I shook my head and pointed to the beach. 'URGENT. Can you come?'

'What kind of urgent?'

I thought about that. Were there levels of urgent? Wasn't urgent just urgent? To make sure, I said, 'Super extra extremely urgent.' Even though it was slightly less urgent than it had been before, because Henny and Nathaniel were at the beach, so at least the eggs were being protected.

'Right.' Tom put his shoes on in about five seconds – which, for the record, is exactly what I call a jiffy – and said, 'Back soon, Jo.'

I was thinking, *Uh-uh – doubt that when you find out what's going on down there.*

He closed his front door. 'Tell me what the problem is,' he said, as we set off.

I got to the main part of the story and he stopped. 'Leatherback eggs?'

'Yes,' I replied. 'Leatherback eggs.'

His mouth fell open, but not in a good way.

He didn't believe me. Obviously.

42. NATHANIEL

I couldn't believe my mother had done something like that. 'Is that why Grandma was furious with you?' I asked.

'That and other reasons. When you were a baby, my life was messy. Then your father left and I was a wreck. You were difficult: you couldn't bear noises, smells, bright lights. You hated getting wet and clothes that were tight and certain foods and – well, lots of things. You needed order and routine, and I didn't have any. Still don't, but I'm trying to change that. Grandma said I couldn't look after myself, never mind you, and she filed for custody of you. Rather against my will, I'm afraid. She was an incredible woman and an excellent grandmother, but you were *my* son.'

Her voice was shaking.

'Why didn't I come to live with you?' I asked. 'In India. Or anywhere.'

'She wouldn't allow it, Nathaniel. She told me I'd have no case, so not to bother fighting her. She said she was doing what was right for you. But I didn't know how much I'd miss you. It became harder with time, not easier.'

I felt uneasy, knowing Grandma had done that. I didn't understand it at all.

The day Grandma died, the head of my prep school had stood at the door of my classroom and called my name. I picked up my coat and she led me to a taxi. Grandma was lying in her hospital bed with her eyes closed. The pinkish room smelt of cleaning products and medicine. Aunt Nancy and my mother were each side of her, crying. Uncle Charles stood behind Nancy with his customary blank face, and nodded in a manly way when I walked in.

My mother's lips trembled and she shook her head. 'Just gone,' she whispered, wiping her nose. 'She said to tell you she loves you.'

'Why didn't you get me sooner?' I asked, numbly. 'I wanted to say goodbye.' But nobody answered.

Remembering that made me feel very uneasy, so I said, 'One of my favourite ocean facts is that the Mariana Trench in the western Pacific Ocean has a deepest point of around 36,000 feet, and the other is that two-thirds of sea life is yet to be discovered.'

My mother smiled. 'And that is exactly why, when I met Ivy, I thought of you. I knew you'd see her around – you can't exactly miss her – but I didn't want to leave it to chance. She's the most wonderful girl – full of life. Entirely her own person. Doesn't care what anyone thinks of her, and she has a deep love for animals. Like you do. More than that – she has an affinity with them.'

'What do you mean?'

'I did some reading and there are animal communicators all over the world – some might be fraudsters, but some are the genuine article. She seems to . . . understand them.' She smiled and added, 'Who knows? But that's why I sent you to the library that day. So you two would meet. Jeremy and I thought you'd be so good for each other.'

I felt awkward that she'd engineered our meeting, so I said, 'Leatherbacks swim as far north as the Arctic Circle, but they don't nest here.'

'Not under normal circumstances,' she said. 'But those circumstances seem to have altered. So now we need to protect her eggs and make sure they hatch.'

43. IVY

'Eggs? Impossible.'

Tom the vet made a squinty face and looked like a grumpy grizzly bear. It didn't help that chest hairs poked up from the neck of his T-shirt like he had a furry creature stuffed down there.

'I know!' I cried. 'But it's actually very possible, because there they are, on the beach. In *danger*. So please could we hurry?'

He didn't hurry. In fact, he stopped walking completely, which is the very opposite of hurrying. 'Listen, missy. It's the middle of the night. I'm tired, my wife's tired, and you woke us both up for nothing. I'm not in the mood for this.'

He turned around and started walking home.

'No! Please!' I yelled. I bit my bottom lip and tried not to cry. I was so fed up with having to explain myself to people who didn't believe me, or laughed at me and made fun of me. Even though I pretended I didn't care, it hurt. So I said, 'I can communicate with animals. I can, whether you believe me or not, and I promise you a turtle has just laid her eggs on the dunes.'

Did he believe me?

Well, what do *you* think?

'Henny's there,' I added, 'and she'll tell you it's true. So will you please call all the people and organizations you'd call if you *did* believe me?'

He blew a raspberry, but – you know – gently. More like a horse's whinny.

'Fine. Let's take a look. If it's true, then, of course. And if it isn't, you are in so much trouble.'

44. NATHANIEL

'The trouble is,' I said to my mother, 'I can't leave tomorrow. Not now. Could I . . . stay with you longer?'

I didn't know why that would be a sad thing to hear, but she smiled in a way that made her lips crush inwards. 'Thank goodness for that,' she said. 'There's nothing I'd like more. I'll call Charles and Nancy in the morning. Nathaniel, I always wanted you. Always.'

I looked up at the milky sky and said, 'OK.'

'Really.'

'OK.'

We sat for a minute in silence, looking at the shimmering sea. Beams from the lighthouse flashed like searchlights across the sky, but they were dimmer tonight in the bright glow of the moon. I liked lighthouses. There might be over three million shipwrecks on the ocean floor, but there would be a great many more without lighthouses. And I was pleased they were electric now and not lanterns fuelled by whale oil, like they used to be, because I liked whales too. Blue whales' voices have got deeper in recent years but no one knows why. I don't know if I like that or not. I suppose it depends on the reason.

I felt awkward about this conversation, so I said, 'In Northumberland in 1838, a lighthouse keeper's daughter called Grace Darling rowed out with her father into a storm to save nine people on a sinking ship.'

'I know this has been difficult for you to hear,' my mother said. 'Grandma did an excellent job of bringing you up. But I'm your mother and I'd rather like my job back. If you'd like that.'

Above us, because of the moon, I could only see the lights of two stars. On a dark, clear night, depending on where you are, you can see up to 20,000 stars, and for about 19,000,000,000,000,000 (or 19 quadrillion) miles, the approximate distance to Deneb in Cygnus. Deneb is bright enough to be seen virtually anywhere in the inhabited world. But this was a full-moon night and I didn't know I could see Deneb.

'If you did want to stay with me,' she said, 'permanently, I mean, then perhaps you could attend a day school rather than board. Everyone's always boarded in our family, but I'm quite happy to break that tradition. Then you could see your father again. If you wanted to. He'd love to get to know you.'

'If he doesn't try to hug me.'

'I'll be sure to let him know. And you could help me greenify the house. I really do feel that to have any hope at all, we need to fundamentally change the way we live. We could do the things you mentioned: install solar panels, collect rainwater—'

'Grow organic vegetables,' I said. 'Go plastic-free.'

'Use the water pistol instead of toilet paper . . .' my mother added, and laughed. 'It doesn't have to be a water pistol. There *are* other washing options.'

With really bad timing, she held out her hand and said, 'May I?'

She wanted to hold mine. I didn't want to be touched, but I was willing to try it because she was being kind and I wanted to be kind too. Plus, other people made it look straightforward.

I held mine up awkwardly. She touched my fingertips with hers and then flattened her hand so our palms were touching. It was warm and close, and I didn't like it.

'OK,' I said, and took my hand back.

She smiled. 'That's more than enough. Truly. I could not have asked for a better son. Tom.'

'A better son *Tom*?'

'No, no – I meant you ... but ...' she pointed at Ivy, who had had just come into view with a huge man in shorts showing large calf muscles, who I assumed was Tom, the vet.

45. IVY

Tom the vet turned on the torch on his smarty-pants phone and, very carefully, considering he was massive and had hands like bear paws, he pushed back the surface of the sand. 'Crikey O'Reilly! These look like—'

I rolled my eyes. *Why oh why does no one ever believe me?*

'—'course, I'm no expert,' Tom went on, 'so I'm not sure which species of turtle laid these, but—'

'Leatherback!' we all said at the same time.

He sucked in his breath like he'd eaten the chilli hidden in the middle of a fruity chew (not relevant). 'I very much doubt that – I need to call the Marine Conservation Society. What time is it? Not sure anyone'll answer, but . . .'

He trailed off, stood up scrolling, and paced along the beach. People who walk while staring at phones look like they're being controlled remotely by someone who isn't very good at remote control. Henny, Nathaniel and I stood watching him in the fresh night air with the full moon above and a bunch of leatherback turtle eggs buried in the sand beside our feet.

'Peter, it's Tom Rosten. I know – middle of the night – sorry. But it looks like a turtle's nested on the beach in Southwold . . . I *know* it's impossible, but I've seen the eggs. Possibly a leatherback, but . . . no, I *know* they don't . . . no, I *know* . . . but they're definitely a sea turtle's. Uh-huh. OK. OK. Sure.' He hung up. 'I need to send some photos.'

The camera flash made me blink bright lights again and again on the inside of my eyelids, like a guinea-pig disco in my head (not relevant). Half a minute later, his phone vibrated and he answered the call. 'Uh-huh. *I know!* I have no idea! 'Course. Call me back.'

'What?' I asked impatiently.

'He said they look like leatherback eggs. They're going to send experts immediately to verify it.'

I looked at Nathaniel and turned my pupils inwards.

'Incredible. Well, whatever they are, we need to protect them – close off the beach, bring teams down to monitor them.' He looked up in disbelief. 'This really is the most unbelievable discovery. For a sea turtle to nest in these shores is—'

'Impossible. Yes, we know,' I said with exasperation.

'Guys, you've done an awesome job – really – but you don't need to stick around now,' he said. 'We'll take it from here. Henny, why don't you go ahead and take the kids back to bed? I've got this.'

I put my hands on my hips. One of the most annoying things about being eleven is that whenever anything important happens, adults always shoo you away like you're irrelevant, and then take over. Even if you're the one who found it. Why do they do that? You're one person and they're one person so you're just as important and relevant as they are, just a bit shorter. Sometimes you're *more* important if you have a skill. And I had a skill. I had more than one skill, obviously – not everyone can ride a bike with a crate on her head. But I had a skill that could help the turtle and her babies. Not that anyone would believe me.

When I'm an adult, I'm never going to do that. I'll never treat children like they're irrelevant or less important, just because they're smaller than me. And I'm going to believe everything everyone tells me, no matter how weird it sounds. Although I might have to rethink that later because it doesn't seem like a very sensible strategy.

'Absolutely not,' Henny said, making me love her more than any human female alive. 'This is Ivy and Nathaniel's discovery and they will remain very much involved in whatever happens next. We're not going anywhere.'

I wanted to hug her again but I just nodded maturely.

As we waited for Tom to do whatever he was doing, we listened to the symphony of the sea. It's so loud, especially at night. It makes a deafening *kkkr-rrrush* but at the same time, over there, there's a mellow *hurrrrsh* followed by a saggy *shumpshhh*. A hissing *pssshhhh* on the left, a *yoummmsh* in the middle, a *pshuttt* and then a *crummppssshhh* with a *drrrrrush* on the right. I closed my eyes and listened and then opened them to watch the moonlight dancing on the waves in white frothy spewlets. That's not the most beautiful word, but it is one of my favourites. Martin always makes me feel so small, but at the same time, full of excitement, like anything can happen.

'As if *they've* got anything to do with it,' I grumbled. 'I was the one who was singing and saw her come up on the beach.'

'You were *singing*?' Henny asked, surprised.

'My singing isn't that bad.'

'No, no, you see, my mother studied a tribe in Mexico called the Seri, who believe that leatherbacks are sacred. They hold that in ancient times, leatherbacks and people understood each other and communicated freely.'

''Course they did,' I said. 'Bet no one believed *them* either.'

Henny smiled. 'Although that skill's been lost, they do think that leatherbacks still understand songs and speech. So now, if a fisherman sees one, he alerts the village, and everyone drops what they're doing and gathers on the shore to sing the turtle in with special songs.'

'Really?'

'Yes, really. Once it's ashore, they hold a four-day ceremony and then sing it back to sea. And when the eggs are ready to hatch, they sing to the hatchlings to send them safely into the ocean.'

'So maybe the turtle came *because* I was singing?' I said. (I didn't mention that I was singing to the jellyfish.)

'Possibly.' Henny sighed. 'Ivy, I'm afraid we're the reason those eggs are on this beach. My sister Nancy and me.'

And she told me the maddest story I've ever heard.

At the end of it, Henny said, 'It seems all three of you have found a home here.' She glanced at Nathaniel. 'At least, I hope so.'

He didn't answer, but he's not great at understanding things unless they're said really clearly and directly.

Henny squeezed my hand. 'It's time to call Nancy,' she said. 'I have a rather enormous apology to make, and some incredible news to give her. She'll be delighted. Even if it is 1 a.m.'

46. NATHANIEL

Calling Aunt Nancy at 1 a.m. wasn't normally acceptable. Grandma said you shouldn't make calls after 9 p.m. or before 9 a.m. unless it's a life-or-death emergency, but my mother said this qualified as one.

She stood up, brushing the sand from her skirt, gave Ivy the shawl, and walked up the beach with her phone to her ear. 'Charles, it's Henrietta,' I heard her say. 'So sorry to wake you, but could I speak to Nancy, please?'

Ivy was sitting with her head on her knees and the blanket around her shoulders. Tom was looking at his phone screen, which lit his face in a blue hue.

'The eggs have a two-month incubation period,' Tom said. 'If they *are* leatherbacks. I'm just reading up on it now.'

'They *are* leatherbacks,' Ivy muttered into her knees.

'Ivy,' Tom asked, 'what made you go out to the beach tonight?'

Ivy lifted her head and scanned the horizon. 'I felt her coming,' she replied.

Tom squinted at her. 'What do you mean?'

'I just . . . I dunno . . . I felt her . . . out there.' She flourished her hand over the sea. 'She showed me her eggs. I wasn't sure what I was looking at, but I knew she was coming. I tried to tell Nathaniel but he didn't believe me. And tonight, when she got here, I climbed out of my bedroom window and came down to meet her.'

Tom angled his head. He was frowning, but he *was* listening. 'She . . . showed you her eggs?'

Ivy moaned. 'Oh, yes, ha ha – let's all laugh at crazy Ivy who thinks she can talk to animals.'

'I'm not laughing,' Tom said. 'Please. I really want to know.'

Ivy hugged her knees and didn't answer for a long time. Perhaps she was trying to find the right words, or perhaps she was deciding whether to bother explaining it at all. At last, she said, 'If I make my mind go really quiet, I can . . . kind of . . . *zshoom* into animals' minds and they can *zshoom* into mine. I focus on them and get this . . . information. Sometimes I see images. Sometimes I feel sensations in my body or hear sounds in my mind. Sometimes I just *know* something.' She pushed her hair off her face. 'It helps that I love them and would never harm them, and they know that.'

'I see,' Tom said, rubbing his chin. He couldn't see. I couldn't either. 'Well, if this turtle is a leatherback, she's going to come ashore and nest many times in the next few months,' he said. 'We're going to have to close a long stretch of the coastline near here. She may well have nested on neighbouring beaches already.' He tutted. 'If she has, how will we know where the nests are?'

'Ahem,' Ivy said. 'I can help you there.'

Tom looked at me. I don't know what his look meant.

'I really can,' Ivy said. 'It's irrelevant whether you believe me or not.'

My eyes felt bleary and dry but I didn't want to leave the beach. Footsteps in the sand behind me made me turn my head. 'She coming,' my mother said, walking back with her phone in her hand. 'With Charles. They'll be here in a few hours.'

47. IVY

An hour later (during which time Henny went home and made us two hot chocolates *each* — RELEVANT: when has anyone ever made you two hot chocolates in the same hour?), Dr Peter Richardson arrived from the Marine Conservation Society. He was with a bouncy woman in blue who said her name was Dr Julie Wood and a woman with blonde hair who introduced herself as Dr Irina Ramage. They bent down, frowning importantly, checked the nest with expert fingers, and then confirmed that the eggs had been laid by a leatherback. Which, duh, we already knew.

Then they stood up, shaking their heads, and said it was absolutely, utterly impossible for leatherbacks to nest in the UK. Except it was evidently quite possible after all, which is what I'd been telling everyone all along, if they'd only believed me.

The marine conservationists called up other expert-y people and they turned up, too, and for some reason, lots of them had beards. The women didn't, but *they* wore men's clothes. Not the kind of shirts I wear, either: more like big T-shirts with animal charity logos under fleeces also with animal charity logos, knee-length shorts with lots of pockets (and probably animal charity logos) and hiking boots with red ankle socks, even though another boiling-hot day lay ahead and they weren't going hiking. It was all very interesting, but to be honest, not particularly relevant.

I was more tired than I'd ever been in my entire life by then. I hadn't slept all night and my body didn't like me any more. I could tell.

After an hour of standing around eating sandwiches with actual sand in them, the sun rose and hung on the horizon like a luminous egg yolk. Above me, runner-bean clouds were yellow, orange, pink and purple and the sky was pale and shy, as if it were stepping out for the first time, which I suppose it was. For today anyway. The gulls above cawed in long, thin cries, making everything feel even more stretched out than it did already, and screeched jokes at me, trying to wake me up. It didn't work. Their jokes are really bad, to be fair.

Sand was between my toes, and as I sat feeling the grittiness, the beardy people brought heat lamps out of their vans and complicated gadgets for measuring and calculating, then cordoned the area off with ropes, plastic bollards and stripy tape.

All along they talked about how impossible it was that this impossible thing could happen and how bizarre it was that it was possible, and all I could hear was mutter mutter climate change, mutter mutter rise in upper-ocean temperature, mutter mutter decrease in sea-ice growth and mutter mutter we may be witnessing a new colonization event. I couldn't understand their scientific jargon but I got the drift.

Henny sat beside me, her eyes red and her crazy hair dancing around her face with the sea breeze. 'Time for bed, I'd say. For a few hours, anyway. Let me walk you home.'

My stomach sank. This rumpus was bigger than the biggest rumpus I could ever have imagined. How was I going to keep a low profile now?

Henny walked me to my gate. 'Do you want me to come in?'

'I'd better go by myself,' I said, thinking it would be less rumpus-y that way.

Daddy Rufus curled up in his bed and fell asleep right away, which is what I'd like to have done. Jeremy was in the garden and when I walked out, Dot ran to me clucking. Boy, did I have a story for her.

'I'm planting a wildlife resort for creatures,' Jeremy said. 'Are you all right? You look exhausted.'

I burst into tears.

'Hawthorns,' he said gently, 'crocuses, forget-me-nots. To attract bees and whatnot.'

'Thank you,' I snivelled. He might not have been as warm as Rufus, my dog father, but he was a kind man, and bees desperately needed humans as kind as he was.

'And over here, cornflowers, lavender and pansies to attract butterflies.'

I nodded, my chest feeling as warm as a lump of fudge melting on a visiting vicar's chair (not relevant). 'But I was just . . . at the . . . beach and something humungous has happened—'

'Oh dear. Not a rumpus, one hopes.'

My soul shrank. 'Well . . . yes . . .'

Aisling stood at the patio doors.

'I see,' Jeremy said. 'A big one?'

I went white as a swan on a frozen pond and tried not to panic. 'Huge.'

'Oh dear.'

'I know. I'm so grateful to you both, really I am. You've given me a home and I don't want to be taken away. But a leatherback has laid her eggs on the beach and she asked me to help them survive.' Tears streamed down my face, because I loved Jeremy and Aisling but I would have loved them quite a lot more if they believed me, even just once, because not being believed is the worst thing ever.

'Then you must,' Jeremy said, his eyebrows ferreting around.

'I must . . . what?'

'Help her.'

'Absolutely,' Aisling said. 'You must help everyone you can. We all must. Isn't that right, Jeremy?'

Daddy Jeremy nodded and smiled. 'Ivy always does,' he said. 'And if she says a turtle has come, then a turtle has come, and although that *is* rather a large rumpus, it's certainly a valid one.'

I bit my lip to stop it wobbling. I felt so much love for them, I almost exploded on the spot.

Henny appeared beside me, and said, 'It's true. Bizarre and outlandish as it sounds. Please allow me to explain.'

48. NATHANIEL

'Could someone please explain from the beginning?' Charles said. He stood beside me, asking lots of questions, as Nancy and my mother talked without shouting or getting cross, and then they hugged, which I'd never seen them do, not even at Grandma's funeral. Then my mother cried and apologized, and Nancy did, too.

I didn't understand why they were so emotional, and I don't think Uncle Charles did either, so I said to him, 'A schoolgirl near Bristol called Mya-Rose has been identifying and recording bird species since she was nine. She's identified nearly five thousand birds and she's only sixteen.'

He frowned and stood up. 'How is this going to work, then? From now on, I mean.'

It worked like this:

To allow the turtle peace and space to come ashore and nest again, the council closed the dunes, the beach and a few miles of coastline in either direction so they could check for other nests.

For the next eight weeks, around thirty vets, conservationists and scientists camped near the eggs on the dunes, and at five other nest sites they found with Ivy's help, because for some reason she had an uncanny way of knowing where the other nesting sites were. They bustled about setting up equipment, fiddling with it and drinking from flasks that made their breath smell of coffee. Monitoring machines were connected to laptops, and even though it was a hot summer, huge lamps lit and warmed the beach day and night to ensure the incubation temperature remained constant.

They built long runs from the nests to the sea, and cordoned them off with ropes and sticks so no one would tread where the turtles were going to make their dash to the water. Although the scientists and conservationists took responsibility for the eggs, they let Ivy, my mother and me set up camp on the dunes beside them.

Every morning, Irina greeted me and shook my hand as if I were an adult and an equal, which I liked almost as much as the fact that tiny frogs lay their eggs in rain-filled elephants' footprints. We only slept there sometimes, because it's hard to sleep with people talking until late, and although my mother brought me a comfortable camp-bed mattress, my duvet, a pillow, my rucksack and my torch, Huntington House is six minutes, thirteen seconds' walk from there, and I don't like being uncomfortable, so I slept there most nights.

We even swam in the sea, my mother, Ivy and me. This was our chance to swim with a turtle, even if she'd already moved on, and I felt as if she and I were . . . bonded . . . somehow.

A line of onlookers came, many with their dogs on leads, and asked questions, then sat with fish and chips on benches as if the event was a long, ongoing movie.

It was exciting.

I liked it very much indeed.

49. IVY

I like being on the beach in the dark, with the wind in the trees and someone unzipping zipping their tent and wispy clouds floating across the moon like they do in films about werewolves, which I didn't want to think about. We camped there most of the summer, although they completely took over because we were only children and our beards weren't long enough and we didn't wear enough fleeces. If the collective noun for turtles can be four words – a bale, a nest, a turn or a dole – then the collective noun for male scientists could be a *beard*, a *fuzz*, or a *hairy leg*, and for females a *fleece*.

At least Nathaniel had finally found someone who was interested in his random facts. He and Irina had conversations that went like this:

Irina: 'Do you know, when the Dumbo octopus is shy, it can wrap itself up in its tentacles.'

Nathaniel: 'What *I* like best is that its brain is wrapped around its oesophagus, so it can't eat anything too big or it'll explode its own brain.'

Irina: 'That IS cool.'

Then they found some other weird fact to share.

I promise you, that's what they were like.

The scientists were so impressed with how much Nathaniel knew that Irina said he could do work experience in the Marine Conservation Society when he's older.

You should have seen his face.

Sitting on the beach on those long summer evenings, time slowed down and stretched out. I tried to imagine the world before we put roads and shops and traffic lights on top of it, when it was all soil, grass and trees, and filled with animals.

Under the big, clear sky, I felt tiny but part of something huge that I couldn't explain or understand, and it felt so good to be part of it. If you ask me, my skin isn't the outline where I end and the rest of the world begins. There are no borders between me and everything else. Life is just one big whirl of colour and smell and noise that somehow includes me.

While the adults talked and zipped their tents a gazillion times, I sat looking out at Martin and talking to the turtle, who was on her way back home. I felt the echo and hum of deep open emptiness and an inner push to keep going. I heard a flap and a lap, and I saw endless blues dotted with sprinkles of sunlight. And I felt how happy she was to be getting out of those freezing grey waters near that little island where that nice girl lived who was kind to animals and knew just how they felt, because long ago, she'd once been a duck.

For the rest of the summer, I slept on the beach half the time, and the other half, took care of my bee hotel and the animals that needed help.

Meanwhile, Nathaniel spent most of his time at Henny's. He's not very good at camping, even with half his bedroom in the tent. Together they sorted out their house, which if you ask me was long overdue. That house was full of junk. Their long-term project is to make it eco-friendly, and they probably wash their butts with water pistols, but to tell you the truth, I never ask because I don't actually want to know.

And then, one night at the end of August, it happened.

50. NATHANIEL

It was night and I was asleep when they knocked at the door. My mother came to my room and said, 'Nathaniel. It's time.'

Moonlight flooded into my room through a gap in the curtains. I kicked off my thin sheet, dressed in a T-shirt, shorts and my anorak, checked the blue ball was in my pocket and ran downstairs.

The front door was open. Ivy stood on the doorstep, her huge shirt, red wellies and dark hair surrounded with the orange glow of the street lamp. I could tell she was smiling even though I couldn't see her face clearly.

We climbed in the back seat of Tom's car and my mother sat in the front.

'This is it, Nathaniel,' she said. 'Imagine how excited Grandma would have been.'

I was grateful to my mother for saying that,

because despite everything, I wished so much that Grandma was there to see it.

As we approached the cordoned-off run, I saw Irina bending over near the nest with a thermometer. 'Oh, great!' he said. 'You're here. The sand's moving. Look – see where it's dipping slightly? There. It's slow, though. It's been seven minutes already.'

The sand had a dimple about five centimetres wide. A PhD student called Ralf was filming it with a video camera, and Julie, Tom and about fifteen others were filming it on their phone cameras. Every five or six seconds, sand fell in and the area around it cracked, deepening the dip.

Irina and I stood behind the cordon watching. Not far away, the others stood chatting, laughing and filming. The lighthouse beamed white flares across the sea and I stared at the sand, which was moving as if it were breathing.

'Why do you think leatherbacks have soft shells?' Irina asked me.

'Because they're so large?' I suggested. 'Males can reach 2.6 metres, and weigh 900 kilos.'

Irina replied. 'Yes, on a turtle this size, a bony shell would be heavy and it would find it difficult to rise to the surface of the water, never mind walk on land. Having that soft, flexible skin means their lungs can expand to take in more air so they can dive to deeper depths in search of food. They can dive deeper than 4,100 feet! But we think its soft shell might also have to do with temperature regulation, or diet, and— oh, they're here.'

I turned my head.

Camera crews – one with BBC, one with ITV and one with SUFFOLK NEWS written on the sides of their vans – were parking on the road beside the beach.

51. IVY

Why is the news only ever about humans? There's a whole planet of creatures trying to survive brutal murder and shameful torture and all types of devastation and *that* never gets reported on the six o'clock news. If a healthy giraffe gets put down in a European zoo, that might cause outrage and get a slot on the news, but a whole species dying out? The slaughter of five more elephants by poachers? A captive female leopard that refuses to eat because her cubs have died? Ohhh, nooooo. *Their* lives aren't worth talking about. I tell you something, if *I* ever become the prime minister or the head of TV, I'm changing that.

That day, though, the news wasn't only about humans. My discovery was being broadcast all over the world, and everyone was waiting for the first eggs to hatch.

'Ivy! Look!' Nathaniel cried.

The well got slightly wider, and then, just as the film crews started talking to their invisible audience through the camera, the first tiny flipper poked out of the sand and everyone started whooping and cheering. In that little patch of the world, tiny creatures were starting their lives, and what they needed more than anything was encouragement and love. So I started singing, which made the news crews smile, but I'm not sure if they were smiling *at* me or smiling *with* me. Because apparently, that's a thing.

Julie, Irina and Ralf sang with me. Nathaniel had told them about the Seri, and they must have thought, *Well, why not?*

I'm not sure the Seri sing Abba or High School Musical songs about all being in this together, which is what Julie and Irina wanted to do, but I don't think it mattered. The little turtles came out of the sand all the same.

52. NATHANIEL

First, wing-like flippers surfaced from the sand. Then heads, eyes closed, followed the flippers, then wriggling limbs and finally turtles, a few centimetres long, confused and tiny, emerged groggily as the adults yelled much louder than Ivy or me, 'Look! They're coming! They're coming!'

The first one came out facing in the wrong direction, but did an abrupt U-turn and dashed along the run lined with humans towards the sea. The mass of collapsing sand turned into a swarm of tiny body parts as more and more came out. They looked sugar-dusted, their flippers huge compared to the rest of their bodies, and as the watching humans cheered them on from the sidelines like spectators at a race, Tom started counting.

After five, seven, ten had appeared from the small circle of sand, they came out so fast, he had trouble counting them. They stood on each other, climbed over each other and put flippers around each other as if they were hugging and supporting each other. Some were jostled upside down in the rush, others scrambled the wrong way and then reorientated, their wings rotating like wind-up toys, until they reached the frothy waves and slid into the sea.

All the while, my mother stood arm in arm with Nancy, both with expressions on their faces that I couldn't really read because they seemed joyous and anguished at the same time. I thought of Grandma. Somehow, even though she wasn't here any more, she'd brought her family back together again. Perhaps that's what she meant when she said something was here for me. She'd given my mother back to me, and me back to her. I had a new home. I'd swum with a turtle. And I had a friend.

I looked over at Ivy. She was singing awful songs to the hatchlings with a few of the conservationists, while the others whooped and clapped until there were just two left in the hollow. One was upside down, its flippers going back and forth as it tried in vain to turn itself over, and a very weak one was having trouble climbing out.

We got closer. Some of the scientists were saying 'Awww,' and laughing, but I didn't find it funny. Those last two hatchlings couldn't do it on their own. They'd die if we didn't intervene.

'Why are we just watching? We need to help them,' I said to Irina. I didn't like to see them struggling. Especially not when we were standing right beside them and we could help.

Irina shook her head. 'Watch.'

With immense effort, the upside-down turtle flipped over. There was great applause and cheering, but the last one, alone and frail, didn't have the energy to pull itself up.

'It won't make it,' I said.

'Keep watching,' Irina said, squatting down to knee level.

Slowly, with great difficulty, the weakest hatchling heaved itself up and out of the well, as if it were very old instead of very young. By then it sounded as if a football team had scored a goal – everyone was cheering, clapping and hugging each other. I stood back in case anyone came towards me, and watched with great concern as it waddled clumsily along the run until, eventually, it too disappeared into a wave.

I stared at the sea, blinking with concern, knowing all those tiny creatures were in there. Scientists were on boats, putting sargassum weed into the sea for them to feed on, but still.

I turned to Irina and squeezed my blue ball (I mostly left the red one at home these days). 'How will they make it?' I asked.

Irina paused. She has bright blue eyes and a Russian accent and she comes to Huntington House for a shower and crumpets and tells me lots of facts, so I like her.

'You know,' she said, 'only one in a thousand turtle hatchlings survives to adulthood. Eggs are taken from nests, and there are so many air and sea predators that most don't survive the race to the water, or their first few weeks when they get there – and that's in the tropics where the water is warm. Never mind the nets and plastic they battle with once they're adults.'

'That makes me feel worse, not better.'

She smiled. 'But leatherbacks are ancient – they've been here over a hundred million years. They've made it this far. We have to hope they can keep going.'

My head felt as if it were being crushed. The hatchlings faced uncountable trials to survive and even if they did make it to adulthood, the issues they faced were overwhelming.

'It's too late, isn't it?' I said quietly.

She paused, checking what I meant. 'For them?'

'For the planet.'

Irina blinked and drew in a long breath. 'You

know, Nathaniel, one of my favourite quotations is from a beautiful book written by a scientist called Carl Safina,' she said. 'The book's called *Voyage of the Turtle*. In fact, I printed the quotation out and stuck above my desk. It goes: *Turtles have taught me this: Do all you can and don't worry about the odds against you.*' She paused, and then added, 'Those tiny hatchlings have so little chance, but they do everything they can to survive anyway. And that's what we need to do. We can't lose hope. The odds against us are enormous, but we have to do everything we can. And keep doing it. You understand me, right?'

I nodded.

'Look.' She pointed at Tom, who was lifting Ivy on to his shoulders, and like that the news crews interviewed her. They called me over too, and that's how our small, private, family story was broadcast across the whole world.

53. IVY

That was the funnest night of my whole life (I'm not sure funnest is a word but I like it so who cares?)

As the sky turned from spoooooooky blue to slightly bright, then mellow yellow to boom-pow-shakalaka blue, hundreds of people came down to the beach, including Gus, to see where the impossible possible had happened. They stood behind the cordons, chatting and taking photos, and I kept an eye on Gus as he scanned the beach with mischief in his mind, just in case he tried any funny business. I do not trust that boy one bit.

The beach remained closed so the scientists could test and measure who-knows-what, and cough and stroke their beards and nod and frown and tell the news crews what they could and couldn't do, and where they could and couldn't stand as they fiddled with cameras and huge fluffy microphones.

At breakfast o'clock, Jeremy and Aisling arrived. At first, they stood to one side, looking bewildered. I gulped. I had caused the most ginormous rumpus. But Jeremy didn't look at me in *that* way at all. Instead, he opened a large Tupperware box and stepped forward to the cordon.

'Would you like . . . ?' Jeremy asked, handing Aisling's home-made scones to the scientists and vets (and us). 'Yes, please do take for your colleagues . . . of course you may have another . . . Ivy, these three without raisins are for you.' (He knows me so well.)

'Remarkable, Ivy,' he said, when the box was empty – which didn't take long, to be fair. 'We were extraordinarily proud of you anyway, but now even more so.' His eyebrows ferreted a little above his soft eyes. 'You've saved those creatures' lives, Ivy. That's the most benevolent act a human can do. Even though it caused a rather . . . spectacular rumpus.'

I grinned. It really was spectacular. Nathaniel and I were on every channel on TV. We felt like celebrities, just without piles of money or our own brands of perfume. An over-excited councillor from Waveney District Council said they'd decided to rename it 'Leatherback Beach' instead of 'Bay Beach', which sounded loads better even though she was trying to take all the credit when, um ... HE-*LLO*, I WAS THE ONE WHO SAW IT ALL HAPPEN.

At around lunchtime, Nathaniel and I were sitting in a jeep on the road with its doors wide open, our heads lolling back on the headrests. The car was too hot to sleep in and the beach was too busy, so when Tom arrived and waved me out of the driver's seat, saying, 'You two need sleep. Come on – I'll drive you home,' we agreed, even though we didn't want to go anywhere.

He took Nathaniel to Henny's and me home, and I slept in my comfy bed until four in the afternoon, which is not recommended as you might then be up half the night and then have to find cows, owls and voles to have conversations with in fields across from the house (not relevant).

In the evening, Jeremy and Aisling made baked potatoes with beans for supper, and I told them about the hatching. When I finished, Jeremy's gentle, wrinkled hand reached across the table and rested on mine, and Aisling's rested on top of his. I placed my other hand on top of hers to make a giant hand sandwich.

'You mean the world to us, Ivy,' Aisling said.

Jeremy nodded and blinked kindly. 'I rather think we might retire early,' he said softly, 'if it's all the same with you. All this excitement is a little more than we're used to.'

I felt the same way. It was the first time I was asleep by 7 p.m. since I was about two.

The next day, I went over to Huntington House, and Nathaniel said he had a surprise for me.

54. NATHANIEL

I wanted it to be a surprise, so as we walked to the promenade, I made her put a blindfold on. 'I won't take you there unless you do,' I said.

'But—'

'Blindfold.'

'URGH!'

'Stand there. Outside the door.'

The evening was muggy, and midges jiggled in clouds near our heads. People promenading on the path eyed us inquiringly, wondering what we were up to.

'Ready?' I asked.

'Can I take this thing off, because it's really driving me—'

'Ready?' I asked again.

'Yes, fine, ready, whatever. Just take it off, will you, so I can—'

I pulled the sheet off the sign, blinked hard, and said, 'You can take the blindfold off now.'

55. IVY

I took it off and blinked hard. After the darkness of the blindfold, the sunlight was dazzling. Interestingly, the beach and my bellyaching sounded three times louder when I couldn't see, like I had my head in a large plastic box (not relevant).

'Look up,' he said.

A white sign stretched across the top of his beach hut, and in big green letters were the words:

The Beach Hut Animal Action Agency.

Helping creatures big and small, and working together for positive change.

No fee unless you're rich.

I grinned.

But then confusion crashed into me like a cloud of locusts on their way to a ~~Carni~~Vegival (not relevant).

'But—' I began, but my mouth was too baffled to even form a question mark.

'I thought you might need a new location. For your agency. I changed the sign a bit. We already have volunteers that want to help. Look at the mural inside.'

I peeked inside the hut. Across one of the longer walls, someone had painted, 'Turtles have taught me this. Do all you can and don't worry about the odds against you.' And underneath, in smaller writing, 'Carl Safina.'

'Like it,' I said, but actually I felt a little bit like crying.

Nathaniel pushed his glasses up his nose. 'Good. We have work to do.'

As the sun went down, our shadows became long as lampposts and our arms looked ten feet long. I sat next to Nathaniel at the door of the hut, looking out to sea, watching the sky turn from velvet-rose-red to knee-bruise-purple and Jaffa-orange-orange. Some pesky mosquitoes near my ankles were hoping for a tasty blood supper and I was telling them off when I had an idea.

I waved them away, a little conflicted, because if any creature deserves a splatting, it's those guys. 'It's hard to save the world when you're eleven-ish,' I said.

Nathaniel nodded. 'Agreed.'

'Especially when people don't believe you.'

'Some things are hard to believe,' he replied in a serious voice. 'Great white sharks can sense tiny quantities of blood in the water three miles away, and penguins actually have knees.'

I laughed and waved the mozzies away. 'I guess sometimes you've just got to believe. Like those cuuuuute little turtles. We don't know how to save the world, though. Look how big it is.'

'Step by step – that's how. Irina said if we do everything we can whenever we can, that's already a good start. 'Least until we get older and can work in conservation or sustainable energy and *really* make a difference.'

I nodded, even though *I* was planning to be a professional animal communicator and have a side business making fudge. I didn't say that. Swollen white welts on my ankles itched. I'd been someone's burger and fries. I should have kept my wellies on.

'We'll set up the most efficient and pro-active animal action agency we can,' he said.

'That sounds very unexciting.'

'Not at all. We'll start by doing things at home. Here, in Leatherback Beach.'

'Good idea. We'll invite people to bring me their

troubled pets. I'll make sure hamsters have better homes, dogs have better sniff options and squirrels have nuts in winter. And I'll teach you how to talk to people so they don't walk away from you thinking you're weird.'

He frowned. 'Do people think—'

'Yes, Nathaniel. They do.'

His face looked extremely serious again. 'I see. Well, that would be good, then. Thank you.' He paused and added, 'I was thinking more of keeping beehives, writing lobbying letters and educating people on sustainable homes and clothing.'

'Yee–sss,' I said, cautiously. 'Of coooourse we'll do that stuff.' How was he not getting bitten? I spat on my finger and rubbed it on my bites. I wanted to get my wellies on, so frankly, I'd have agreed with anything right then.

Over the next few months, Dot and I helped a dying lady see her horse, Cornelius, one last time (it was Cornelius's idea), and watched Mr Galloway taking Clyde almost daily down to the harbour and across the fields, stroking him lovingly. To be fair, Dot didn't do much, but she insisted on coming so I took her along.

Life changed after that. People came to the beach hut with their pet problems, big and small. Percy came to teach people about hamster care and happiness, Gus came to gawk and laugh but at least he came, and Tom the vet did, too. Mainly because I saved at least one parrot's life after she swallowed a pink plastic doll's shoe (long story) and translated from pig that Bessie the Potbelly's infected tooth wasn't her only issue: she was also in pain from a nail in her toe. Pigs aren't the easiest patients. Tom reckons leash-trained pigs that sit or lie down on command, have been on car rides and know their names are much better patients than 'wild child pigs' whose owners give in to their needs, so I know what *I'll* be doing if I ever have a pig as a pet.

Nathaniel organized weekly beach cleans, made posters to slow motorists down near hedgehog crossings (my idea), wrote letters, protested outside businesses and supermarkets, took a course in energy efficiency, went to a lab where scientists were working on affordable substitutes for plastic, and built a small motel for tired insects in his mother's back garden.

Just before Christmas, around the time 'The Beach Hut Animal Action Agency' went from being in the newspapers to being on TV, and branches like 'The Garden Shed Animal Action Agency', 'The Damp Garage Animal Action Agency' and 'The Hove Park Animal Action Agency' started opening first across the country and then across the world, Nathaniel received an invitation. It was from Irina, asking him to take part in her conservation project in Africa the following summer (relevant – but that's a story for next time).

Nathaniel replied saying he'd go, but only if I could go too because we came as a team. I was so happy he said that because *umm, hello, AFRICA!* Although I think I'll have to swot up on random facts or I'll have no one to talk to.

I tell you something, he's a good friend, that kid.

LEATHERBACK TURTLES

The earliest known turtle-like creatures appeared around 220 million years ago; sea turtles around 200m years ago; and the type of sea turtles we would recognize now, around 100 million years ago. Leatherbacks evolved in the Cretaceous period, along with the dinosaurs, around 110 million years ago, making leatherbacks the closest creatures we have to living dinosaurs. It is believed that during the Jurassic period, tens of millions of them swam in the waters of the Earth. Scientists believe an asteroid hit the Earth 65 million years ago near the Gulf of Mexico, causing an ice age that killed the dinosaurs along with 85% of Earth's species. But some sea turtles survived, and two families of turtles survive still: hard-shelled turtles, and leatherbacks. The DNA of modern leatherbacks is so closely related to each other, scientists think one small group survived, and that all leatherbacks on Earth are descended from that one small group.

Of all turtles, leatherbacks are the record-breakers. They are the largest, heaviest (weighing as much as a ton), fastest, cover the most distance (crossing entire ocean basins), and swim the deepest. But the master navigators are not extinction-proof. According to the

Leatherback Trust, 'just 6 percent of hatchlings will survive their first year.' (www.leatherback.org) Those that do grow to adulthood face the biggest problem of all: man. Oceans are changing, sea levels are rising and the beaches they nest on are eroding or covered in waste. People still eat turtle eggs. Turtles are caught in fishing gear, eat plastic bags, or are eaten themselves, and their ocean habitats are polluted, as is their food.

Between 1980 and 2000, the world lost 70% of its leatherback population. Thirty years ago, there were 115,000 leatherbacks in the world. Now there are around 36,000. In the Pacific, the number has fallen from 90,000 to 5,000. Estimates by the WWF suggest that there are only 2,300 adult females Pacific leatherbacks left, making it the most threatened of all marine turtles. We are in danger of losing the biggest and most beautiful turtles of all.

However.

A number of nations and communities around the world have set up initiatives to protect turtles and their eggs. Between 2016 and 2018, volunteers picked up – by hand – 13 million kilograms of knee-deep plastic from Versova Beach in Mumbai, India, in what the United Nations called 'the world's largest beach cleanup project'. Spearheaded by a local lawyer-turned-environmentalist, Afroz Shah, the clean-up led to Olive Ridleys, a vulnerable species of turtle, nesting on the beach for the first time in many years. Volunteers slept on the beach to safeguard the eggs from wild dogs and birds of prey, and the hatchlings made their way into the Arabian Sea in March 2018.

And although leatherback numbers in Pacific have declined 95% in the last two decades, leatherback numbers in the Atlantic are rising.

For the record, leatherbacks do not nest or hatch in UK waters. It's just not possible. Not yet, anyway. But then not all wasp drones are called John and some seagulls tell pretty hilarious jokes.

WAYS YOU CAN HELP

- Ask teachers to incorporate environmental issues into the curriculum.
- Stop using plastic bags and bottles, and ask shops to stop using them too.
- Become a (responsible, balanced-diet, protein-and-vitamin-eating) vegan or vegetarian, or just try to eat more beans and veg.
- Write letters to outlaw pesticides and toxins that kill pollinators.
- Raise money for environmental charities.
- Buy cruelty-free products and recycled toilet paper (or use a water pistol).
- Create a garden wildlife sanctuary. Grow organic food. Plant trees. Use solar and wind energy.
- Pick up litter so it doesn't blow into the sea or get eaten by gulls.
- Foster cats and dogs, or volunteer to help an elderly/working neighbour's pet so dogs can have exciting sniff adventures and cats have someone to play with.
- Keep cats inside at night: they like to hunt and kill many small native animals.
- Walk, cycle or bus rather than drive, and try to travel without flying.

- Have showers rather than baths. Clean your teeth by putting water into a glass. Use a watering can rather than a hose.
- Use less power. Switch lights off when you leave a room. Switch off the computer, TV or radio if you are not using it.
- Reduce food waste and make less rubbish. Try to avoid buying fruit and veg in packaging. Make a compost heap or start a worm farm to use up food scraps. Recycle.
- Monitor your carbon footprint and paper usage.
- Learn about – or even work in – conservation and ecology.
- Use a glass and a postcard to rescue spiders safely from corners.
- Carry a carrot and an apple (to treat bored horses and donkeys), dog treats (to get dogs to move, come or stop biting someone's leg), bacon rind (to reward crabs in the harbour after a hard day of being caught over and over again by feverish children), spare water bottles and some water (for dehydrated gerbils), traps for small animals (to take them to a safer place away from humans and then let them go), emergency nuts and seeds for hungry squirrels and birds, some straw and hay in case of dirty cages, and a rope and a small cardboard box. Not sure why I added those last two, but it seems like a good idea.

SUGAR SOLUTION FOR BEES

Bees on the ground are often weak and exhausted. Sugar water can help.

Add one tablespoon of white sugar to two teaspoons of lukewarm water until it dissolves. Never use honey because most of it is imported and may not suit our native bees. Sprinkle a few drops of sugar solution on the floor beside the bee with a spoon, taking care not to drown it with a big splat on the head. The bee may well thank you for your kindness and ask for the eggcup to be placed among his favourite flowers so other bees can have an energy boost when they get tired. An eggcup is a good size – nothing bigger or birds will fly down for a sugary bath.

ACKNOWLEDGEMENTS

Heartfelt and profound thanks go to the climatologists, conservationists, environmental activists, scientists, charity organizations and individuals who daily try to save what they can, generate positive change for our planet and raise awareness of what more needs to be done. Thanks especially to **The Leatherback Trust** and **The Marine Conservation Society** for the work you do and for providing information to help me write this book. Thanks also to **Friends of the Earth** for sending me links to their Bee Cause pack for Educators, to activities such as planting a wildflower meadow and building bee hotels, and for telling me about Mya-Rose Craig (known as Birdgirl), one of the UK's young wildlife heroes.

After reading *Voyage of the Turtle*, I emailed the ecologist and multi-award-winning author, Carl Safina, to ask for his permission to quote from his beautifully poetic and perceptive book. Thank you so much, Carl, for saying yes, and for your encouraging and inspiring love of the natural world. Your words became the central message of this novel. Thank you to Professor Jeanette Wyneken of Florida Atlantic University and Professor Thane Wibbels of the

University of Alabama for answering my questions on turtle egg transportation, incubation and hatching. Although you both said transportation and incubation were possible but hatching was extremely unlikely, if not impossible, in the UK, I included it anyway because a) I figured, hey, what the heck, b) this is a work of fiction and c) with the world changing as fast as it is, who knows?

Infinite and eternal thank yous, as always, to Hilary Delamere (agent extraordinaire); Rachel Leyshon (editor extraordinaire); Barry Cunningham (publisher extraordinaire); the folk at Chicken House (team extraordinaire); the librarians, teachers and parents who get books into readers' hands (life-changers extraordinaire); my children Luli, Mushk, Mymy and Tushk (offspring extraordinaire); my mother (whom I called 'Ma' which turned into 'Martin' for years, but whose name is actually Mary (matriarch extraordinaire); my excellent and esteemed colleagues at FHS (educators extraordinaire), and Simon Goodrick (train buddy extraordinaire). High five to the real Ivy Pink Floyd, aged twelve (animal lover extraordinaire), for letting me use her name, and to my family and friends who barely saw me when I was doing the (manifold, endless) edits of this book.

Lastly, thanks to all of you, readers extraordinaire: I

hope you enjoyed Ivy and Nathaniel's story. As you know, Ivy is fostered, which means she is temporarily living with people who are not her birth parents. As you may *not* know, Nathaniel has Aspergers. To learn more about Aspergers and how best to support those who have it, please visit

https://www.autism.org.uk/about/what-is/asperger.aspx

or

https://www.aspie.org.uk/what-is-aspergers-syndrome/

DREAM ON, AMBER

She's Amber Alessandra Leola Kimiko Miyamoto (as if the name makes up for her being tiny!)

Amber is half Japanese and half Italian, and is starting a new school with a caveman phone. But the hardest thing about being Amber is that a big part of her is missing.

Her dad.

He left when she was little and if he isn't coming back, she'll have to find a way to make it up to her little sister.

And Amber has a BIG imagination . . .

'. . . a beautifully written story.'
THE INDEPENDENT ON SUNDAY

Paperback, ISBN 978-1-908435-64-4, £6.99 • ebook, ISBN 978-1-909489-49-3, £6.99

DARA PALMER'S MAJOR DRAMA

Dara is a born actress, or so she thinks. But when she doesn't get any part in the school play, she begins to think it's because she doesn't look like the other girls in her class – she was adopted as a baby from Cambodia. So irrepressible Dara comes up with a plan, and is determined to change not just the school, but the whole world too.

'. . . a hugely entertaining read.'
ANDREA REECE, LOVEREADING4KIDS

Paperback, ISBN 978-1-910002-32-2, £6.99 • ebook, ISBN 978-1-910002-66-7, £6.99

WHAT LEXIE DID

Lexie lives in London with her colourful Greek-Cypriot family. She's devoted to her fragile cousin of the same age, Eleni, who has a heart condition. But after the death of their grandmother, Lexie tells a terrible, instinctive, jealous lie about an heirloom necklace, a lie that splits the family apart. It's up to her to bring the family back together ... but after such a lie, can she find a way to tell the truth?

'With a distinctive style, charming illustrations and heaps of thought-provoking moments, What Lexie Did really is a must-read.'
BOOKTRUST

Paperback, ISBN 978-1-910655-46-7, £6.99 • ebook, ISBN 978-1-911077-49-7, £6.99